HAUNTED
LIVERPOOL 17

© Tom Slemen 2012

Published by The Bluecoat Press, Liverpool
Book design by March Graphic Design Studio, Liverpool
Printed by Martins the Printers

ISBN 9781908457035

All rights reserved. No part of this publication may be reproduced, stored in a retrieval system, or transmitted in any form or by any means, electronic, mechanical, photocopying, recording or otherwise, without prior permission from the publisher.

Tom Slemen

HAUNTED
LIVERPOOL 17

THE BLUECOAT PRESS

Contents

Introduction	6
Huyton's Ghostly Viking Ship	18
The Wavertree Death Clock	20
The Coffin	22
The Keyhole Ghost	24
The Old Hag of Old Hutte Lane	26
A Strange Attack on Gerrard's Lane	28
The Birkdale Palace Hotel	31
The Impostors	36
Encounter in a Cemetery	39
Warning from the Future	42
The Haunted Ring	44
Another You	46
An Angel on Mount Pleasant	48
Angels Over Liverpool	50
Bedside Visit in the Royal	56
Gypsy Marie's Fatal Predictions	57
Ho Tay	59
Teleportations	61
The Headless Horseman of Stadt Moers Park	67
Timeslips	69
John Reid of Anfield	79
The Nymph of the Dingle	80

THE SUPERNATURAL TROUBLESHOOTER	83
PARASITIC THINGS	85
THE SERPENT TATTOO	88
THE THREE WOMEN	91
JASPER HECKLING	95
GREMLINS	98
SKIN	100
THE CROXTETH CAVALIER	102
SNOOP	105
MESSENGERS FROM BEYOND	115
THEY ARE HERE	118
THE CRYING GIRL	123
THE HATCHET MAN OF MYRTLE HOUSE	124
PSYCHIC SANDRA	129
THE PROWLER	131
THE MAN WITH THE MOLTEN FACE	134
I SAW WHAT YOU DID	136
WAITING FOR YOU BEHIND THE DOOR	139
GHOSTLY CHILDREN OF LIVERPOOL	147
TURN BACK THE CLOCK	156
OUR HAUNTED SKIES	163
SEND IN THE CLOWNS	167

Introduction

Welcome to the seventeenth volume of the highly popular *Haunted Liverpool* series. When I first started the series I never suspected just how popular my work would become. Like every other Liverpudlian, I had heard ghost stories about my home town and beyond, but never thought of collecting them and researching the subject of Liverpool ghosts, and when I did start putting pen to paper to record the accounts of spooky goings-on, I was shocked by the number of apparitions in this neck of the woods. Then I realised that the dead greatly outnumber the living (by 15 to 1 according to present estimates); just think of all the billions of people who have lived and died before us, and you'll realise what I mean.

Most people in Liverpool have either seen a ghost, had a supernatural experience, or know someone who has had a skirmish with the paranormal. This book looks into stories that were passed on to me, or tales that were the fruit of my own research, and on some occasions, I have even put my own experiences into the mix. Once upon a time I was worried people would think me crazy if I mentioned timeslips or teleportations I had personally been involved in, but now I feel that it's time to come out about these experiences, and so I have included them in this book, and I couldn't care less what sceptics make of the accounts.

The deeper I delve into the world of the occult and the supernatural, the more I realise that the reality we think we know has many layers and planes, and most of the time we only live on one level of reality – until we die of course – and then I believe we enter another dimension of living. Most people are not prepared for this passing over into another realm, and the materialists would prefer to ignore the whole idea of an afterlife. It would seem that all you have is your soul at the end of the day, and in most cases, a person dies and goes to that 'undiscovered country' as Shakespeare put it, never to return to this arena of life. But I know from personal experience that sometimes the dead do return, and there is are a multitude of reasons why they return to haunt us; the main ones being love and hate. The bond of love easily extends beyond physical death, for true love is purely spiritual and can never be destroyed. The same is true of pure hatred, when a person cannot leave this plane of existence because of some unfinished business – usually because revenge has not been exacted – perhaps on the person who has caused someone to die. Maybe some who die do not wish to fully leave this earth for reasons only known to themselves.

Many years ago a man named Jimmy approached me at one of my book-signings and with a very serious look in his eyes, asked me: 'How do you qualify to become a ghost?'

'Through sheer willpower probably,' I replied.

'How do you mean?' he asked, intrigue getting the better of him.

'Well, most people seem to conk out near the point of death, sometimes through pain, or pure anxiety of what lies beyond, or because they are too weak to remain conscious. But if you exercise your willpower each day – focus your thoughts, and perhaps regularly meditate – you will be ready when death comes, barring a sudden violent death, and you will be able to persist, to refuse to move on, and that may turn you into a fully-fledged ghost.'

'Willpower, eh?' Jimmy said, handing me his copy of my book to sign, before saying goodbye and leaving.

Years later I was giving a talk at Woolton Hall on the subject of Jack the Ripper, as unsolved crimes, as you probably know, are another interest of mine. Jimmy congratulated me after the talk, and said a curious thing: 'By the way, you're part right; it is down to willpower.' He had a gleam in his bespectacled eyes, and I noticed an old-fashioned Everton rosette pinned to his lapel. I don't really follow football that much but presumed there had been a Derby or some such game. Then two women stepped in Jimmy's way, and asked when my next book would be out, so I lost sight of him and never saw him again.

Of course, you've probably guessed what's coming next. I later learned through Jimmy's niece that Jimmy had been lying six feet under the soil of Allerton Cemetery on the night I gave that talk. He had died several months previously from a burst lung after a fit of coughing at his home in Crosby. I asked if Jimmy had been an Evertonian, and mentioned his Everton rosette. The colour drained from her face. Apparently Kevin had pinned that vintage rosette to his father's lapel before the lid was screwed down on his coffin, as he had been a blue-hot Evertonian and had kept that rosette from Everton's 1966 FA Cup victory. We come into this life through the birth canal (unless delivered by Caesarean section) and we leave via a rebirth canal in the form of a six-foot hole or a chimney at a crematorium. Whichever route you take, will you be prepared for what lies beyond this life, or have you not given that much thought to that part of your future?

Some of the ghosts in this book are of inanimate objects, such as the spectral Viking long ship that haunts a part of Huyton. These ghosts may simply be projections from the past, and I have catalogued many such 'holograms', for want of a better word. A phantom 18th century stagecoach dragged by two fearsome-looking black horses has been seen tearing up Childwall Valley Road after dark, and a Number 25 single-decker bus from the 1970s has been seen speeding along Grove Street, Edge Hill, in the small hours of the morning, with its interior lit up and its headlights blazing, with not a single soul on board. Phantom planes have even been seen over Liverpool, dating from World War Two, and the solid-looking ghost of a motorcyclist has been seen accelerating down Dunnings Bridge Road, where he seems to crash near Switch Island Leisure Park.

Ghosts of this sort may be as real as the pixels on a computer monitor or the lines on a high-definition television screen, but who or what is generating them is a mystery. Some think nature itself is responsible, and that under certain meteorological conditions, three-dimensional constructs of people and things from long ago are recreated, mere echoes in space and time replayed again and again through forces and conditions of which we know nothing. Primitive peoples must once have thought rainbows and lightning were sent from the gods, but today we know exactly how and why they are generated, and one day, we may unravel laws of nature that will explain mirages from the past that we currently perceive as ghosts.

If you happen to encounter a ghost, what should you do? Well, it's easy for me to say. It's easy to advise 'don't panic' but seeing a ghost can be a very surreal and alarming experience. Our everyday minds are not prepared for people who vanish or appear out of thin air or walk through solid walls. I know many who laugh at the idea of ghosts in the safety of the noon-day sun, but make excuses for joining me on a ghost-hunt on a windy moonless night. Some ghosts are typical attention-seekers, and get up to all sorts of antics just to provoke a reaction amongst the living, but if you face up them, nine times out of ten they will back down. 'Ghosts can't harm you, it's the living you have to wary of,' is an old saying, but poltergeists have inflicted some serious harm over the years, so caution has to be exercised with those types of entity. Ghosts may not be able to inflict physical harm, but budding ghost-hunters with weak hearts should be particularly careful, for I know of two cases where someone has undoubtedly died after being literally scared to death by a ghost.

One such incident took place in the 1990s when a middle-aged Anfield man suffered a fatal cardiac arrest after being chased around his home by the ghastly-looking ghost of a girl. The coroner recorded a verdict of heart failure but I and many others knew the strange truth behind the man's death. He had moved into a house on Anfield, against the wishes of relatives who had heard of the strange goings-on at that address, and one night, after hearing faint screams, the new occupier told the 'ghost' to shut up, thinking it was two girls outside the house messing about. The figure of a girl of about 13 with long black hair and two black sockets for eyes came through the living room door screaming at the top of her voice, and proceeded to chase the man. He ran out of the house and collapsed on the pavement. He managed to tell his neighbours what had happened, then clutched his chest and died. The haunted house in question has now been boarded up for nearly eight years.

There is, I believe, another society all around you – a parallel, secret society of ghosts and entities of which we have virtually no knowledge. I suppose I am a 'ghostfinder' by trade – I find ghosts for a living, although sometimes the ghosts find me first, and even though I have been tracking them down for many years, they can still take me by surprise and they never cease to intrigue me. I do not profess to know all the answers, but I now have a fairly good idea of what is going on in this secret society of spectres and sinister spirits. I believe that you, the person reading these words are a type of 'Proto-Ghost' – a pre-ghost in development if you like. Your body came into creation on the microscopic scale, and after nine months you were born, but your flesh and blood body is only part of the real you; inside you have something else – a spirit, a soul, it has had many names in different cultures at different times in history.

The Buddhist doctrine of *anatta* – 'no soul' – states that the soul is purely an illusion, a figment of the human imagination, yet the Buddhists believe in Reincarnation through Karma, which confuses me. I know there is a soul, and this essence of self-awareness seems to survive bodily death, if the ever-increasing number of Near Death Experiences (NDEs) and Out-of-Body Experiences (including one of my own which I had many years ago) are anything to go by. The one great certainty for everyone is death, and this book should therefore interest everyone, although many people prefer to hide their heads in the sand rather than face that certainty, perhaps because the prospect of death is too frightening. Perhaps you have done something and fear punishment for your 'sin' or maybe you simply fear death because it's still an unknown realm.

I believe that when a person dies, their spirit does one of a number of things. It sometimes goes into a kind of hibernation – the 'rest' referred to in that ubiquitous graveyard inscription: R.I.P. This period of rest might be a day, a month, a year, a century, or even longer. When there is no consciousness there is no time. A person under anaesthetic will not feel ten hours go by during a liver transplant operation. He or she will have not have had the same perception of time as experienced by a wide-awake person on a boring nightshift. For some time then, the dead may, as the Bible says, not be aware of anything: (Ecclesiastes 9:5) 'For the living know that they shall die but the dead do not know anything ...'

It's surprising how many Bible-bashers have told me over the years that there are no afterlife references in the Bible. I say the opposite; it's quite clear that the Bible has many clues to the reality of an afterlife. In the 17th Chapter of Matthew, Jesus undergoes a transfiguration on a mountain, and during this mysterious incident, Elijah and Moses appear. Elijah had the rare honour of being taken up by God to Heaven without physically dying, but Moses died between 1300 and 1150 BC – so his presence on a mountain many generations after his death means there is an afterlife, to Christians at least. The after-life of Moses is just one of many references to life after death in the Bible.

A striking allusion to a spirit returning from 'the other side' is the tale of the Witch of Endor – a female medium who possessed a talisman which enabled her to call up the ghosts of the dead. The story is told in the First Book of Samuel in the Hebrew Bible. King Saul of Israel visits the Witch of Endor and asks her to conjure up the ghost of the deceased prophet Samuel so he could ask him how to take military action against the assembled armies of the Philistines. The ghost was 'called up' but instead of giving King Saul the information he needed, he told him that he would soon meet his death. Saul accepted his fate and died in battle the following day.

Another thing the dead may do is 'wake up' for some reason. Their rest may be disturbed by the living, and this could come about when an occultist attempts to communicate with the dead, such as the type of conjuration practised by the Witch of Endor. This is known as Necromancy, and it was expressly forbidden by the Jews. John Dee (1527-1609) was an English occultist and necromancer extraordinaire who allegedly conjured up the dead many times. In 1605, so the hoary old story goes, Guy Fawkes came upon John Dee and his assistant Edward Kelley in a graveyard one night as they were carrying an exhumed corpse from its grave. Fawkes asked the two men what they were doing, and Dee said he and his companion were taking the body to a secret chamber where he would bring it back to life for a while in order to interrogate it. Dee's disturbing reply captured Fawkes' macabre imagination and he offered to pay him a small sum in return for having a question put to the dead man. Dee was angered by the proposition, as he thought it was wrong to use necromancy to make money in such a way. However, he allowed Fawkes to put his question to the corpse when it was revived with High Magic in the chamber. Fawkes was naturally eager to know the outcome of the conspiracy in which he was participating – the Gunpowder Plot. He trembled when he saw the decaying body sit up on a stone slab in the secret chamber after Dee had drawn symbols and a great circle on the ground around the stolen corpse. By the strange blue glow of Dee's specially made candle, the rotting face turned towards him. The eyes looked liquid, and ready to slide down the mouldering cheeks. 'Will the plot be successful?' Fawkes asked.

The lips of the corpse trembled then slowly parted, revealing a mouth full of foul-smelling brown liquid that dribbled down its chin. In a gurgling voice it said, 'The end will be death for you.'

Fawkes shuddered and stumbled away from the chamber and off into the moonlight. The prophecy of the corpse came to pass, of course, as every schoolchild knows. He was caught after the disastrous Gunpowder Plot, and then tortured. As he was about to be hanged, Fawkes cheated the executioner by leaping from the gallows. He landed head-first and broke his neck. The power to bring the dead back to life is known as 'Anima', and this power also allows a person to pass through walls. The most well-known practitioner of Anima was Jesus, who could go unseen into locked rooms and raise the dead (Luke 24:36, John 20:19, John 11, Mark 16:14).

It would also seem that the soul of a deceased person may sometimes continue with the same consciousness it had experienced before it died. In other words, the person does not go into any dormant sleep-like state after death, but remains as aware as they were in life. I recall interviewing a man named Doug who was involved in a car crash in Cheshire many years ago. He was speeding along a street one evening when he hit a bollard. Doug had seen a friend drown when his car went into a canal and he was unable to unlock his seatbelt, so Doug never wore one again. So when he hit the bollard he was catapulted straight through the windscreen in a split second by the force of the impact and found himself travelling along the tarmac at 50 miles per hour. He rolled to a halt and got to his feet, astounded, as he had suffered no injury. He walked back towards his car and saw someone lying in the road, about 50 feet from the vehicle. His hands and face were a bloodied mess and his limbs were obviously broken. The crash survivor then realised with utter horror that he was looking at himself. He had somehow come out of his body. He paced up and down in shock, and even watched the police and ambulance arrive, then everything went out of focus and Doug woke up almost 24 hours later in intensive care. The transition from life into 'death' for him had been seamless.

What other states of consciousness do the dead experience? Many ghosts are earthbound because of concerns for the living; empathy with a person or persons left behind. A mother or father may not pass on fully because they have strong emotional bonds to a son or daughter; a husband may not be prepared to pass over after death because he longs for his wife etc. Some ghosts are the spirits of people who haunt a place because that place featured so heavily in their lives, and it's not unusual to hear of ghosts of former members of staff haunting shops, offices, factories and so on. There is a certain boiler-suited ghost that haunts a factory in Kirkby who is known to be that of a workman who died on the premises many years back. He keeps returning to his workplace, perhaps because his job meant so much to him when he was alive. This type of ghost is sometimes little more than a 'sleepwalker' – not reacting to people who challenge them, and simply acting out the routine they carried out like clockwork when they were in a nine to five job. The consciousness of such a ghost may be very similar to the type of limited consciousness of a person who is experiencing a dream during rapid-eye-movement sleep.

In rare cases, demonic entities, known in the Occult as Cohorts of the Infernus, will come from the region we (largely ignorant) mortals call Hell, and for some sinister ulterior motive, they will mimic a dead person, but their impersonation is always far from perfect.

Many years ago I investigated a case where a woman went upstairs in her house after hearing her young daughter call her name, but when she reached her room, the child was sitting on the edge of the bed, staring at the wall. The mother asked her what the matter was, then glanced through the window and noticed her real daughter in the garden. Sensing that the 'thing' on the bed was not her daughter, she left the bedroom quickly. This was probably a case of a demon impersonating a member of the living for some reason which at present, remains inexplicable.

Irresponsible dabblers in the Black Arts congregated in Anfield Cemetery in the 1960s, and tried to conjure the spirit of a demon into a dead body they had dug up. Before they could complete the ritual, the police turned up and the occultists fled. The body was re-interred with a minimum of publicity so as not to upset relatives of the dead person, a woman in her sixties. A week later, the solid-looking ghost of that woman was seen walking through Anfield Cemetery in a fog, and was initially assumed to be someone visiting the grave of a relative, until they saw that she was wearing a burial shroud. A doctor visiting his wife's grave encountered the ghostly woman, and she showed him her stitched up post-mortem seam, which stretched from her stomach to her cleavage. 'I live again,' she declared, tears of joy trickling from her eyes. The doctor was a fairly religious man, and suspected that the ghost was some demonic entity. 'There is only one life after death,' he said, looking the apparition sternly in the eyes, 'and that is the eternal life with Jesus Christ. Do you agree?'

The face of the woman seemed to morph into that of something almost reptilian and hideous, and it turned away and flitted back into the mists. The doctor was convinced that a demon had taken on the likeness of some dead person in order to convince people that life after death was possible, even without Christ. That was his belief, and that is the conviction of many Christians. Could the aforesaid tale have any bearing on the following little tale, related to me by a number of people many years ago?

Every amateur local historian knows that Liverpool's Anfield Cemetery opened in 1863 and had its very first internment in May of that year – 77-year-old Margaret Place – but very few people know about the cemetery's catacombs, excavated in four sections some 25 feet below the graveyard clay and strengthened with thick sandstone arches and walls. Sealed up there for eternity is the wife of a 19th century Russian nobleman, bedecked in the finest jewellery, some of which was created by the celebrated Peter Carl Fabergé. Up until 1958, some fascinating people, many of them visitors from exotic places, were interred in the catacombs, but let us go back to the swirling, freezing fog of December 1961. The fog was so dense that ferries collided in the Mersey and people were allowed home from work an hour early as the city's ice-slicked roads ground to a standstill. Elderly night watchman Stan Kidd bravely kept a diligent watch on roadworks from his 'sentry-box' hut on Priory Road. Stan sat swathed in a tartan scarf, sipping rum-laced tea from a chipped enamel cup as he squinted into the embers of the coal in his brazier. The time was approaching 9.40pm, and from the corner of his eye he saw a procession of silhouettes in the fog flitting past – towards the cemetery gates, which were now closed.

Stan left his hut, took a short walk into the grey vapour void and caught a glimpse of what looked like two men in long robes, scaling the cemetery gates with lightning agility. As he stood there, wondering why on earth anyone would want to go into such a vast place of the dead on a fogbound night, a gloved hand landed on his shoulder. The old 'cocky watchman' yelped, then turned to see it was only the policeman Fred MacArthur on his cemetery-circling beat. 'Put the kettle on, Kiddy,' said the jovial young constable, lighting a Woodbine. Stan Kidd was glad to see his friend, and he threw a wooden crate into the brazier and set the whistling kettle on top. A chatty cabby soon joined them: John Wood, a mutual friend, who was soon hogging the brazier. Stan found him a cup, and they started to talk as the fog thickened. At half-past midnight a woman in white – in Anfield Cemetery – was seen by all three men, gazing shrunken-faced through the gates, dressed in what looked like a burial shroud. Reaching through the railings she mouthed silent words. PC MacArthur and cab-river John Wood reluctantly went to see what she wanted. 'Where am I?' she whimpered, looking confused. She collapsed. The two men scaled the railings and tried to help her but found she was more bones than flesh. Then three panting policemen turned up inside the cemetery and told PC MacArthur that 'nutcases' in black cassocks with swords and other paraphernalia had broken into the catacombs and removed a woman's corpse before fleeing, but the body couldn't be found. 'I didn't see that,' said the cabby, looking down at the crumpled corpse. He scaled the gate in shock and left. The woman, who had died in Edwardian times, was re-interred without her living relatives being traced and informed.

There are other types of ghost too. Some are not real, in the sense of possessing a degree of consciousness, but are little more than images from the past (and sometimes the future). Our understanding of what we call Time is very feeble, but sometimes time may revert to a certain period in a particular location, so that a 'phantom' tram may appear out of nowhere and trundle down a modern street. These timeslips are more common than people realise, and I have investigated and documented dozens of them. Time may also occasionally flip forward, so that a person who has walked into the time-shifted zone can see and hear future events. Some say that a few UFO reports are merely glimpses of the vehicles that will be flying around in our skies in decades to come. There are a number of ghostly vehicles haunting Britain's roads, some of which seem to be sent or manipulated to act as an omen.

Locally, we have a ghostly single-decker bus that sometimes hurtles down Grove Street from Toxteth in the early hours of the morning, its interior brightly lit and headlights glaring, yet there is never a single passenger to be seen in the vehicle, nor a driver at the wheel. Why this bus is seen is anyone's guess, but some linked its appearance to a number of accidents in the 1970s involving buses at the zebra crossing at the Myrtle Street junction. Many people cannot accept an inanimate object such as a bus having a 'ghost' because it does not have a soul, but I believe that the bus is not a ghost with a consciousness, such as the ghost of a person who has died, but a construct of some disembodied intelligence, which remotely-controls the vehicle for some unfathomable reason.

One of the best documented cases of a spectral vehicle is the ghostly red double-decker Number 7 bus that haunted St Mark's Road and Cambridge Gardens in the North Kensington area of London in the 1930s. The ghost bus was seen by many people during its reign of terror, and on several occasions the vehicle caused accidents, including one where a motorist died when he swerved to avoid the bus and hit a wall. Some believed the phantom bus was trying to warn the authorities of the blind corner at the junction of St Mark's Road and Cambridge Gardens, a black spot where numerous fatal accidents had occurred over the years. At around 2am, one witness told police: 'I was turning the corner of Cambridge Gardens and I saw the bus tearing down towards me. The lights on the top and bottom decks, and the headlights, were full on, but I couldn't see a sign of any crew or passengers. I yanked my steering wheel hard over, scraping the roadside wall, and the bus just vanished.'

At the inquest into the motorist's death, an official from the bus depot swore that he once saw the eerie bus draw up in silence in the middle of the night, long after all the other buses has ceased running. The double-decker then faded away into nothingness. Dozens of locals who had seen the ghost bus wrote to the newspapers and the coroner's office, offering to give testimony at the inquest. In the end, the authorities decided to demolish a wall at the haunted junction and widened the road, after which there were no further sightings.

Did something 'project' the double-decker on to the roads around the dangerous junction to highlight the hazard of the blind corner? If so, who or what was the projector and where is this entity located in relation to our three dimensions of space? The Projector is just one of the unknown members of the invisible society that surrounds us in space and time, and perhaps is responsible for the hologram-like vessel which is documented in the very first story in this book ...

Tom Slemen

Huyton's Ghostly Viking Ship

In November 1965, gales lashed the British Isles, leaving a trail of death and destruction across the nation, and Liverpool, being a port, was blasted from the Irish Sea. Vans were overturned on the dock road, and the Canadian Pacific liner, the *Empress of England* was stormbound at the Gladstone Dock up in Bootle. All the ferry services were suspended, including, of course, the Isle of Man ferry, as winds of 117mph were recorded, and all flights out of Speke Airport were cancelled after a plane was blown off the runway. A whirlwind was witnessed on Lime Street, and it brought down scaffolding, injuring five people, and a plasterer at work on a building on Lime Street was left clinging to a ledge, 40 feet in the air, for ten minutes, until a ladder was found. A woman with an umbrella was actually picked up by the whirlwind on Church Street, and deposited on the awning of C&A. A meteorologist from Liverpool University witnessed the woman flying into the air like Mary Poppins, and had never seen anything like it. There was talk in the papers about the freak weather being the result of someone – possibly the Russians – testing out an H-Bomb near the north pole, because for a fortnight before the hurricanes of 1965, people in Liverpool, Manchester, Preston and other northern towns, had reported seeing a strange green glow in the northern skies at night. There was even a report in the *Liverpool Echo* of people in Kensington, Everton, Aintree and Formby being able to read a newspaper by the light of this green glow, and an expert told the *Echo* that the glow was not the Northern Lights. So what was it?

When the glow was at its most fierce, something very strange happened in Huyton that has never been explained. That week in November 1965, a policeman named Steve was on his beat in Huyton, at around 11pm. He passed Hambleton Hall on St David's Road on the borders of Page Moss and Knotty Ash, and being a Saturday night, Hambleton Hall was crawling with teenagers, because it was a venue where groups such as The Beatles, The Searchers and others played. There was a scream, and Steve saw a black man run away from a group of girls. One of the girls said the man was known only by his nickname, Ego, and he had tried to rob her purse. The girl also claimed that Ego had 'tried it on with her', so the policeman ran off after him. Ego ran south, crossing Liverpool Road, down Woolfall Crescent and on to Twig Lane, where Steve almost caught up with him, but Ego suddenly outdistanced him and bolted down Rupert Road. Steve kept up the pursuit, and finally, on Archway Road, by the railway bridge, Ego stopped, exhausted, and leaned against a wall, expecting to be arrested. Steve was also exhausted, and as he approached Ego, said, 'Come on, lad.'

'Officer, I've never been in trouble in my life. That girl asked me for a light, then started screaming.'

'You can tell me all this at the station.'

All of a sudden, both men noticed a green glow in the sky which lit up the railway bridge, and what they then witnessed was incredible. In the green glowing cloud that formed in front of them was the black silhouette of what was obviously a Viking long ship, and it came gliding along through the air as crackling bolts of electricity came off it. The ship ploughed through the road and pavement, and gradually lit up in colour, illuminating the huge square sail, and about 20 men sitting on deck, working the long oars. Ego backed away, because he was the closest to this strange apparition, and all he could say was, 'Jesus Christ!'

Seconds later, the Viking ship faded into nothingness, and the green cloud along with it, leaving a strong smell of ozone in the air. Ego was taken into custody, but later found to be completely innocent. The girl who had made the accusations was found to have a record of false claims in the past. Steve happened to mention the phantom Viking ship to a colleague, and he in turn told someone else, and as a result, Steve was hauled before his superior, who advised him to see a doctor. When Steve insisted he was telling the truth, he was told he would be dismissed on medical grounds unless he stopped mentioning the 'ridiculous' incident. A detective quizzed him a few days later, and asked him to give an account of that Saturday night. Ego said, 'Did the officer tell you about the ship we saw?' Then gave a blow by blow account which matched Steve's story in every detail. Even so, the detective still dismissed the whole incident as an optical illusion.

Forty-five years later, Steve contacted me and told me what he and Ego had seen, and I researched the incident. I discovered that in 1828, a gang of Irish navvies working for the railway engineer George Stephenson, were making excavations for the foundations of the railway bridge on what is now Archway Road, when they discovered the remains of a Viking ship. Archaeologists were baffled as to how a ship, over a thousand years old from Scandinavia, could be found 15 feet underground in the middle of Huyton. The clue was the River Alt, which ran close to the site of the railway. It's now known that the River Alt was much wider thousands of years ago and a huge lake existed in Huyton, where the Hag Plantation now exists. Sand has also been found beneath Huyton, proving it was once a landing place for ships in ancient times. I have also had many other reports about the ghostly Viking ship being seen on Archway Road over the years, which seems to indicate that inanimate objects can also have ghosts.

THE WAVERTREE DEATH CLOCK

If you need a reminder of the shortness of your life, look at a clock, and imagine if you will, that each five minutes measures a decade of your life. You are born at noon and, if you are lucky enough to reach the age of 75, which is currently the life-expectancy of us Westerners, then you'll be dead by the time the clock reaches half-past seven, and it's probably already later than you think. The clock is an attendant Grim Reaper, cutting us down, not with a scythe, but with its sweeping hands. If ever a clock was synonymous with death and misfortune, I would say it was the Picton Clock which has surveyed Wavertree with its four faces since 1884, when Sir James Picton presented it to the locals as a memorial clock, dedicated to the memory of his late wife Sarah, who had passed away in 1879.

Over the years a strange apparition has haunted one of the dials of this clockwork tombstone – a ghostly human face which supposedly heralds doom and misfortune. The earliest report I have of the spectral visage is from 1954, when several people noticed that something looked 'wrong' with the western face of the clock – the one looking down Wavertree High Street. At the time of this incident – around 9.15pm, the clock faces were illuminated by dim orange lights, but the western dial seemed to have a series of blemishes upon it that slowly materialised into an eerie-looking four-foot-tall face with beady eyes. On seeing the face, an old woman from Prince Alfred Road made the sign of the cross. She had seen it before, she said, and had lost her young sister that same night from pneumonia. About 20 seconds elapsed before the face slowly vanished. The next day, three young girls returning from the Magnet cinema, a few hundreds yards from the Picton Clock, went to the Wavertree High Street to buy sweets. As they attempted to cross the busy road to go home, a taxi screeched to a halt a few feet away from them. The cab driver shook his head, smiled, then gestured for the girls to cross, but a bus overtaking the taxi didn't see them and hit the third girl, pinning her under its wheels. She died from shock. A few of the locals believed the ghastly face which had appeared on the Picton Clock the night before had been a kind of omen to the tragedy.

About a month afterwards, at midnight, Teddy boy Frank Hokerift was returning from his girlfriend's house on Eastdale Road, on his way home to Childwall, when he too saw the face appear on the clock facing the Wavertree High Street. A car travelling up the street slowed, and the driver popped his head out of the vehicle's window to get a proper look, as he thought he was seeing things. He shouted to Frank, 'Hey, mate, can you see that face up there?' Frank nodded. The driver swore and said, 'Thank God for that, I thought I was going doolally. What the devil is it?'

Drinkers coming out of the Coffee House pub saw the face too, before it faded away a minute later. Within an hour, a car crashed near the roundabout on which the clock stood, and the driver's body was thrown through the windscreen, landing with a sickening thud on the pavement outside Jenkins the undertakers ...

THE COFFIN

On the Saturday night of 31 October 1981, at 10pm, 19-year-old art student Louise went into the Cambridge pub, within a stone's throw of Abercromby Square. She bought cheese and onion crisps and a half of lager, then sat on her own as the autumn gales spattered the pub windows with rain. It was Halloween, and the eerie intro from the Special's doom-laden hit, *Ghost Town*, was coming from the jukebox. Louise was feeling very lonely. She had just fallen out with Vicky, her friend at uni, so when an old flame came into the pub, she was very glad to see him. Paul Dickson was 21, and now worked as a trainee butcher in St John's Precinct. He'd been on a pub crawl with his docile mate Simon, and they'd both been stood up by two girls who had promised to meet them in Chaucers on Hardman Street. 'It's their loss ... they're the losers,' Paul reassured his meek-looking friend, who was still going on about being stood up. And then Paul noticed Louise, and he was as pleased to see her as she was him. He sat at the her table with Simon and they chatted about old times and caught up on what was going on in each other's lives. Another friend of Paul's came in with his girlfriend and joined them. With it being Halloween perhaps, their conversation turned to the paranormal.

At this point a young black lad of about 18, known only by the nickname Montserrat, his Caribbean birthplace, joined in the conversation from a neighbouring table and turned out to be a font of weird tales. He told the tragic story of 15-year-old Candi Sue Wiser, whom he had known when he lived in the States. In 1977, Candi Sue became very depressed after her boyfriend dumped her, and on Halloween night she idly spelt out her name in 13 Scrabble tiles and asked the spirits to help her. As Montserrat and the girl watched, something shuffled the 13 tiles around until the chilling reply was spelt out: 'Suicide Answer'. Candi Sue later hanged herself – according to Montserrat, but Paul didn't believe him. The barmaid who had come over to announce last orders commented that some anagrams seemed inherently wicked. 'You get a weird sentence if you rearrange the letters in the word "desperation",' she told the group, 'you get "a rope ends it!"'

'There's this coffin in an old empty house, right,' said Montserrat, 'and if you look at it on Halloween, you see the body of the next person who'll die this year, honest.'

Paul had had enough of the lad's ridiculous claims, and slapped his hand down on the table and said, 'Right, I bet you a tenner you're a liar! Show me this coffin. Go on, show me it. Right now!'

Montserrat accepted the wager and led Paul, Louise, Simon and the couple, out of the pub and into Toxteth, until they reached a secluded poorly-lit street. There stood a derelict house which could only be accessed via a manhole to the cellar. The youths crawled down the hole to explore the house and there, sure enough, in the musty attic, was an empty coffin resting against the wall. The group sat, as directed by Montserrat, and Paul rolled up old newspapers into a makeshift torch and lit it. Three times, Montserrat said: 'Spirits of Halloween, show us who will be the next to die.'

The moon slid from behind a rain-cloud and shone its faint blue light through the attic window. Six pairs of eyes were trained on the moonlit coffin, and for a few minutes, nothing happened. The newspaper torch went out, and the snaking smoke from it travelled towards the coffin and began to twist about impossibly until it formed the image of a girl. Everyone gasped. The gaseous figure was at once recognisable to Louise as her best friend Vicky, and she screamed. Louise fled the attic and in the pitch black descended the rotting stairs. She tried to climb out of the cellar manhole but Paul had to help her up. That night, Louise visited Vicky and told her about the coffin apparition but Vicky closed the door in her face after accusing her of making the tale up so she could get back with her.

A week later, Vicky died in a car crash.

THE KEYHOLE GHOST

Ghosts feature many times in my books, but what are they? In most people's minds, ghosts are assumed to be visitors from a supernatural realm. Statisticians say that around one in five people now believe in ghosts and around one in ten claim to have seen one. I would say that in Liverpool there is a much higher incidence of ghostly encounters.

From my research over the years, I would say that there are several common myths about ghosts. They don't always appear after dark, and are often encountered in broad daylight, sometimes looking as solid as you or me. One obvious give away is outdated clothing, but phantoms of the recently-departed usually wear contemporary clothes. The shroud-draped shade is just a corny caricature. Another myth is that ghosts can't harm you, yet poltergeists have seriously injured many people by hurling objects at them and lifting them bodily into the air. Many years ago, one man in London was thrown out of a second floor window by a poltergeist and almost broke his neck. I once investigated a poltergeist in Speke and had a nail driven through the palm of my left hand. The nail flew out of the cupboard door under the stairs of the haunted house and hit me with the force of a .22 pellet. I still have the scar as a souvenir. Poltergeists have also caused fires, and may be at the root of the occasional blazes which defy explanation. The sudden appearance of a ghost can cause traumatic shock and may even trigger cardiac arrest in a susceptible person. So ghosts can physically harm you, although most are benign.

There is a chilling exception in a certain hotel in the north west. In the early 1950s, a beautiful young blonde woman who was also a prostitute, nicknamed Pippa, booked into a certain room at the hotel in question with a client. The client, a married man in his fifties, found himself so stricken with guilt, he couldn't go through with the sex act and left the hotel room. About five minutes after he left, Pippa heard someone laughing out in the corridor, and she peeped through the keyhole to see what was going on. No one was there, but something passed the keyhole twice. Suddenly something sharp and long was thrust through the keyhole, piercing Pippa's left eyeball and passing deep into the tissues of her face. The tip of the object, which seemed to be a knitting needle, emerged at the top of her right cheek. Pippa collapsed and was taken to hospital, now blind in her left eye. She told the police that her client might have carried out the act, perhaps as some warped act of revenge for coaxing him to the hotel. The police couldn't trace the man, and probably never bothered looking anyway, because Pippa was just a 'common prostitute' in their eyes.

About a month later, a couple in their forties – June and Charles Bragg, booked into the hotel, and occupied the room where Pippa had had her eyeball skewered. At around 1 o'clock in the morning, June Bragg woke up after hearing laughter outside her door. It sounded male despite being rather high pitched. She listened at the door, and after a few moments the laughter stopped. Then she felt an excruciating pain in her left wrist. When she looked down she saw that a long hat-pin, or perhaps a knitting needle had been thrust through the keyhole straight through her wrist so that it came out of the other side of her arm. As she screamed, the needle was withdrawn back through the keyhole.

Charles Bragg leapt out of bed, yanked open the door, and dashed out into the corridor. No one was about. The couple went to the reception desk and reported the incident to the old man on duty. He had seen no one go into the elevator or pass him on their way to the stairs. The police were notified, and an investigation began. The hotel manager admitted that, as far back as the late 1940s, there had been similar incidents, where someone had tapped on doors or caused a commotion, and that same person had then thrust a long needle through the keyhole, obviously intending to injure the guests. The needle attacks continued for another three years, only ending when the hotel was refurbished.

The hotel manager and a bellboy were walking down the corridor one evening when they heard footsteps approaching. Something neither of them could see brushed past the manager, and he felt something sharp pierce the back of his hand. A spot of blood appeared at the point where something invisible had stabbed at him, and then the eerie footsteps were heard running away down the corridor.

I have investigated this strange case in some depth now and will publish my findings and theory in a future publication.

THE OLD HAG OF OLD HUTTE LANE

So many have seen her yet no one knows who she is – or was. One evening in the summer of 1982, Paul, Marty and Sarah, all aged 14, left their neighbourhood in Halewood on their BMX bikes, and headed for a race around Speke's North, South and East Roads, which formed an epic circuit around the Ford car plant. Paul was the self-appointed leader of the trio, and upon this cool and pleasant evening, he almost came to grief on Leathers Lane as he glanced down proudly at his new pair of trainers. A car horn sounded as a car screamed past, startling him out of his inane reverie. 'You plantpot!' Sarah cried out at Paul, afterwards disguising her concern for him with a faint smile. The speeding Cortina-driver beeped his horn repeatedly, even after he had torn past, despite having come within inches of a fatal collision with Paul. The three teens rode down Higher Road then turned right into Old Hutte Lane, a dark and lonely place bounded on both sides by tall thick hedges. The lane had an incline of about 20 degrees, and they struggled with the gradient. The climb left them exhausted by the time they reached the top, where Sarah said a strange thing to Paul: 'Did you see her?'

'See who?' he asked.

Martin, the softly-spoken member of the trinity, murmured 'Yeah, I saw her.'

Sarah and Martin had caught a glimpse of a white-haired old woman in a long black robe on Old Hutte Lane, looking through a long gap in the hedge, her features those of an archetypal haggard witch: wizened and heavily wrinkled, with a prominent hooked nose and projecting chin. In the few seconds they had glimpsed the weird old hag, they had both noticed her stark staring eyes, which were circled with thick black rings. 'What would an old woman be doing standing in a hedge?' Paul scoffed, and then he took off in a burst of speed down North Road, on the first leg of a lap round Fords.

Twilight soon fell, colouring the sky manganese blue, and as the first stars began to appear, Sarah said it was time they went home. She suggested going the long way, via Woodend Avenue, but Paul knew she was scared of going the short way – down Old Hutte Lane, and he called her a chicken. 'I'm not,' she protested, and Paul said Martin was also a chicken, adding 'Yous are just scared cos you thought you saw an old witch!'

'We did see her,' Martin mumbled, 'why would we make it up?'

'Oh, listen to the big "I Am"! Paul isn't scared of anything, so let him go home that way then!' said Sarah.

'Okay then, I will. It's true, I'm not scared of anything!'

And to prove his point Paul rode off towards Old Hutte Lane. Martin and Sarah went the long way home, but when they got to Halewood, there was no sign of Paul. A motorist later came upon him lying unconscious in the road on Old Hutte Lane. He had bruise marks on his throat and a deep crescent-shaped bite-mark on his shoulder. All Paul recalled was an old woman jumping out at him from the hedge on Old Hutte Lane. The sight of her face, which was a mass of wriggling maggots, caused him to pass out. He was treated at Whiston Hospital and given a tetanus injection because of the shocking bite to his shoulder.

For weeks Paul suffered lucid nightmares about the old woman, in which he could see every squirming maggot crawling out of the holes in her pock-marked face. When Mike, the boy's uncle heard about the attack, he turned cold, for when he was Paul's age, back in the 1970s, he recalled how, one night, he had been out riding his Chopper bike with a group of friends, and they had all been chased by an almost skeletal woman in a long black robe with a grotesque, disfigured face. Mike hadn't seen the face close up, unlike his best friend Alan, who had told him that it had been 'dripping with maggots'.

I have received quite a few letters, emails and telephone calls (to the studios of Radio Merseyside when I have been on air talking about the paranormal) about the old hag of Old Hutte Lane and she seems to have quite a history, but I can find nothing to account for her antics nor why she should haunt that particular part of Halewood. I have heard widespread rumours (there are always rumours about this type of ghost) that she is a witch who was put to death for bewitching the lord of a local manor. What manor could this be? Well, there may be a clue in the name of the lane which the weird figure haunts – Old Hutte Lane.

The Old Hutte was a moated half-timbered 12th century manor house which once stood on the site now occupied by the Ford's car plant. From 1291, the occupiers of the Old Hutte were the Ireland family. The grand three-storey residence stood alone in the fields of Halewood on a square island surrounded by a deep moat. In 1952, Liverpool City Council promised it would renovate the Old Hutte but decided to demolish it because it was supposedly riddled with dry rot, but surely they could have replaced the centuries-old timber? Perhaps there is some truth in the stories about the old hag of Old Hutte Lane being the vengeful ghost of a witch who was put to death by the inhabitants of the local manor. Some witches were left to rot after they were hanged from a gibbet, and perhaps this is what the maggots signify. We may know more one day.

A Strange Attack on Gerrard's Lane

In the late 1950s, a Halewood couple in their twenties drove to a party in Longview, near Huyton. In those days, drink-driving was not frowned upon the way it (rightly) is now. If you drink and drive today, and you're above the legal limit, you'll be fined, banned, even imprisoned, but the breathalyser wasn't used in the United Kingdom until 1967, and initially many breweries, motoring organisations and civil liberty groups strongly opposed it. In the late 1950s, it wasn't unusual for a policeman to help a drunken person staggering from the pub to his car and advise him to get home to bed and sleep the drunkenness off.

Will and his girlfriend of two years, Susan, had had a bit too much to drink at the party in Longview, yet Will drove home to Halewood in his Vauxhall Cresta Saloon with Susan at his side telling him to drive slowly as she felt sick. Will stepped on the accelerator and deliberately tore off, thinking it was funny. Neither wore a seatbelt. Today, we don't think twice when we belt up before a journey, but in the 1950s, despite the high number of road deaths, there was very little attention paid to safety. One leaflet in that day and age even advised motorists in the event of an impending collision to 'slide on to the floor and crouch with arms between head and instrument panel'.

Anyway, as the Vauxhall tore down Gerrard's Lane, it spun out of control and hit a wooden post. Susan was thrown through the windscreen, and Will was hurled sideways out of the car, along with the driver's door, and ended up in a ditch, out cold, with the door on top of him. Susan sustained a broken right leg, broken left arm, and minor head and neck injuries. She lay there in the road, and in those days, that part of Gerrard's Lane was a very dark and secluded place, the only light coming from the moon. Susan tried to move, but she was in agony, and lay there in the stillness, thinking for a few moments that it was all a dream. Accident victims often report this feeling of unreality. Then Susan heard gentle footsteps approaching, and she thought, thank God, someone must have seen the crash. I'll be okay now. She wondered what injuries Will had suffered, and she wanted to blame him for speeding, and causing the crash in the first place, but she still loved him. Then the rescuer stopped next to Susan and leaned over her. He wore a three-pointed hat on a head of long curly hair, and had a dark scarf wrapped round the lower half of his face. She couldn't see the rest of him because it was too painful to move her head, but it looked as if he had on a thick knee-long black coat. The stranger unwound the scarf from his face – a face so pale that Susan thought he was wearing some sort of theatrical clown make-up, and it made his eyes seem contrastingly dark. He knelt down by Susan, and looked into her eyes as he smiled. His breath was foul, his teeth crooked and dark. His cold hands began to grope Susan, and suddenly he was on top of her, kissing her roughly. She screamed and her assailant clamped his ice-cold hand over her mouth. There was a loud bang. It was Will bringing down the door of the crashed car on to the would-be rapist's head. When people are enraged, or find themselves in life-threatening danger, they can often summon up almost superhuman strength, and lift things they couldn't normally lift. Will lifted the car door high above his head, and grunted as he smashed it down repeatedly on to the bizarre figure until he rolled away from Susan. Will hit him again until the side-window in the door smashed into the attacker's face. The unearthly figure staggered to his feet and ran into the darkness of a neighbouring field.

Susan was crying by now, and Will knelt at her side, holding her hand. There were no mobile phones then, and the couple waited for nearly 40 minutes before Will flagged down a passing car which took them to the nearest hospital. They gave an account of the attacker to the authorities but it was not taken seriously because of the bizarre description.

When they had recovered, Will decided to revisit the scene of the crash, and called in at the Eagle and Child for a drink one evening, and got talking to an elderly man named George who knew everything about old Halewood. George mentioned the stories his grandfather used to tell him, especially about the ghost of the highwayman Toby Gore, who had his hideout near Gerrard's Farm, off Gerrad's Lane, where Will and Susan had crashed. George said a horse-drawn carriage had overturned on that lane in the early 1800s, and the coachman had died of a broken neck. Toby Gore was suspected of raping a female survivor of that crash as she lay in the road. Her name was Susannah Wall. Will's girlfriend was named Susan Hall. Was this just a black coincidence, or history repeating itself? Old George said there had been a number of night-time car crashes near Gerrard's Lane over the years, and some of the survivors had told of an old fashioned man in a tri-corn hat who had come out of nowhere to gloat at the injured and dying.

They say Toby Gore was hanged by one of his own criminal associates, and that he is buried face-down at the junction of Gerrard's Lane, Wood Lane and Winster Drive. One legend says that as Gore was fleeing the scene of rape and robbery near Halewood Farm, the wind blew off his hat, and the criminal's long curly hair became entangled in a huge holly bush overhanging a roadside wall and Toby hung by his entangled hair from the bush as his horse raced on without him!

THE BIRKDALE PALACE HOTEL

Some readers may remember the Birkdale Palace Hotel, which once stood in Southport. Many visiting Hollywood stars and celebrities from all over the world booked in at the luxurious hotel; people like Frank Sinatra, Sammy Davis Junior, Bing Crosby, Fred Astaire, Clark Gable, Boris Karloff, Steve McQueen, Norman Wisdom, Peter Sellers, and Stanley Kubrick, to name but a few. The French-style Gothic hotel was located close to Birkdale golf course, and every year when the Grand National was held at Aintree, people from across the country and the world would swarm to the Birkdale to enjoy its palatial decor and first-class service, its 200 bedrooms, all with hot, cold and specially filtered sea water on tap and, of course, the magnificent seaside views from the hotel.

However, there was a dark history to the hotel that some members of staff and the management knew about, and as much as they tried to suppress them, the weird stories and rumours would occasionally leak out. Since opening, in 1866, it had become a magnet for suicides and murderers, and even in its early days there were reports of ghosts lurking in the rooms and corridors.

The first of these apparitions was believed to be the ghost of one Philip Jones, a sort of upmarket travelling salesman and something of a confidence trickster. In 1867 he went to his room, appropriately numbered 13, and after drinking an entire bottle of brandy, was heard trashing the room. As the manager and several of his staff tried to gain entry to the room, there was a muffled bang, followed by a groan. Jones unlocked the door and emerged with a white hotel towel draped over his head, covering half his face. In a low voice he said, 'Fetch a doctor.'

Blood trickled down from his forehead and down his cheek into his Van Dyke beard. Somehow he was able to explain that he had just put the barrels of two pistols into his mouth, and had blown the top of his head off. His hairpiece was hanging from the elaborate crystal chandelier, and the ivory white ceiling moulding of the chandelier's rose was splattered with the pink and red contents of his brains. The towel slipped off his head, at which a female member of staff fainted, because there was no top to Philip Jones's head. The assistant manager later described how the whole gruesome spectacle reminded him of the way an egg looks when you take off the top part of the shell. One hotel porter standing behind Jones could actually see the back of the poor man's eyes. Mr Jones remained lucid for about a minute, then dropped dead from loss of blood – after saying he fancied a walk along the beach.

Not long after the travelling salesman's death, room 13 was renumbered 12a. Then came the sightings of a dark pillar of cloud that was seen rushing down the hotel's stairs and corridors. Within this cloud, the blood-streaked tormented-looking face of Philip Jones was faintly seen. A priest was brought in to exorcise the entity, and that priest died later that year from consumption. For nearly two years the black cloud wasn't seen, and then in the winter of 1869 it returned. In February 1869 the body of Thomas Lea, an apprentice on one of the Liverpool pilot boats, drowned when his boat was accidentally rammed by the Liverpool Cunard Steamer *China*. Lea's body was washed up near Southport and taken to the Birkdale Palace Hotel, where the inquest was duly held. During the inquest, in broad daylight, a loud groaning sound echoed through the hotel, and the black swirling column of cloud appeared to come out of a wardrobe mirror in one of the rooms. The face of an old man with a white collar was seen in this cloud, and some believed it was the priest who had tried to exorcise the sinister apparition before he died of TB.

In September 1883, this apparition was actually seen outside the hotel on the beach by two archaeologists of the British Association, who were digging close by when they found some rusty old artifacts resembling crumpled crowns. They both saw the shadowy thing watching them as they excavated the sand to a depth of six feet.

In 1885, staff used a ouija board to get to the bottom of the hauntings, and the message said 'stillborn'. The next day, Mrs Mangnall, the wife of the architect of the Birkdale gave birth to female twins who were both stillborn.

On 9 December 1886, a ship called the *Mexico* left Liverpool, bound for Ecuador, and ran aground near Southport at a spot that faced the Birkdale Palace Hotel, and three lifeboats were immediately sent out to rescue the 12 people onboard. The rescue was successful, but at a terrible cost – 27 of the lifeboat crew drowned that day. Their bodies were brought to the Birkdale Palace Hotel and laid out for the inquest. Not long afterwards, disembodied voices, whispering and crying, were heard in the hotel in the dead of night, as well as the distinctive sound of someone retching and of their vomit dripping on to the floor.

Then, in June of the following year, a man named Yates jumped to his death from a top window at the Birkdale after something chased him around his room. As he lay dying, with the tips of his shattered femur bones protruding from the flesh of his legs, he told hotel physician Dr Vernon that a shadow had attacked him in his room. Less than a year later, there was a blazing domestic argument at the Birkdale Palace between wealthy Aigburth cotton merchant James Maybrick and his young wife Florence, after he accused her of having affection for another man. Not long after that, Mr Maybrick died of arsenic poisoning.

Then, in July 1897, we have the strange suicide of 19-year-old Ada Mulholland, kitchen maid at the Birkdale Palace. Miss Mulholland spoke to her friends about the 'thing' which hovered over her bed each night, telling her she was going to die. Miss Mulholland later drank a bottle of carbolic acid. The coroner's verdict was 'suicide during temporary insanity'. Two further suicides took place in the room where Philip Jones had blown his brains out years before, and then in the 1920s, two elderly sisters, named Simpson, were found hanging side by side, both holding hands, both with beaming smiles on their faces. Their joint suicide note said they had both had enough of living and wanted to see what death was like.

On 24 May 1961, six-year-old Amanda Graham, a lovely talkative child, left her mother's shellfish stall in Southport at 5pm and went with a friend to nearby Pleasureland. At a quarter to ten that night, little Amanda was seen sitting on the shoulders of Alan Wills, a 33-year-old porter at the Birkdale Hotel. The next morning, Amanda's body was found under Wills' bed, wrapped up in his underclothes. She had been raped and asphyxiated. Wills said he had no knowledge or memory of what he had done; he had just woken up in bed, seen the body, and panicked. Wills was found guilty of murder and sentenced to life imprisonment.

The hotel never really recovered from being tainted by this horrific child murder, and in 1969 it was demolished, but even the demolition gang encountered all sorts of weird phenomena. Although there was no electricity at the hotel, the lift went up and down of its own accord, even when the cable was cut. After the lift had been battered by heavy-duty sledgehammers, it suddenly plummeted to the basement and embedded itself in the foundations. Whilst staying at the hotel one summer in the 1950s, Frank Sinatra encountered two little girls in old-fashioned clothes standing in the corridor, gazing at him with bulging eyes devoid of any pupils. They vanished in front of him and he ran back to his room to call reception.

In 1980, Stanley Kubrick released one of his most enigmatic and chilling films, *The Shining*, which was a loose adaptation of Stephen King's novel of the same name. Jack Nicholson played the part of Jack Torrance, a former teacher who takes his wife and son to the immense Overlook Hotel, high in the mountains, and empty during the off season, where he will act as caretaker. Overlook is haunted by the ghosts of various murders and fatal incidents which have happened within the building over the years, and the ghosts of these past horrors finally turn Jack Torrance's mind, possess him, and impel him to slaughter his wife and son, just as the previous caretaker had done many years before.

There was a story that Peter Sellers – who had held a lifelong interest in spiritualism and the supernatural – had heard of the many weird accounts of the Birkdale Palace whilst staying there in the 1960s, and he, in turn, told these eerie tales to his friend Stanley Kubrick, who may have incorporated them into his take on the Stephen King novel. A caretaker in the Overlook becomes unhinged and attempts to murder his son, and the caretaker of the Birkdale Palace Hotel murdered a child – Amanda Graham, in 1961. Ghostly twin girls are seen to prowl the labyrinthine corridors of the Overlook, and twin ghostly girl were seen by many – including Frank Sinatra – roaming the corridors of the Birkdale Palace. The phantom twins were said to be two little girls who died there in mysterious circumstances in Edwardian times.

At the end of the Kubrick film, the caretaker of the Overlook chases his son outside into the snow-blanketed grounds of the hotel and is found frozen to death. In the 1870s, a caretaker of the Birkdale Palace went mad during the height of a blizzard and ran out of the hotel with a carving knife, and was later found sitting in a snowdrift, frozen to death. The Overlook in *The Shining* is built on an Indian burial ground, and the Birkdale Palace was said to have been built on a Neolithic burial ground. Perhaps the intriguing parallels between the two hotels are just uncanny coincidences – or perhaps Stanley Kubrick's film is a thinly disguised portrayal of one of the most haunted hotels that was ever graced by the stars of Hollywood in its heyday.

The only surviving part of the Birkdale Palace Hotel is the Fishermen's Rest public house, and that has more than its fair share of ghosts.

The Impostors

In 1984, 45-year-old John Lofthouse suspected his 30-year-old wife Judy of having an affair. She had started wanting to go out without him and when he asked her why, she would say she just fancied going out with her girl friends from work, that was all, and she warned John that his paranoia was driving a wedge between them.

One Wednesday night, in November 1984, Judy went out all dolled up, supposedly for a night-out with her mates, and John decided to follow her. He tailed her to the Grafton, and almost gave himself away at one point, but turned away in time and hid in the toilets. When he came out, he went to look for her again and saw her leaving with Carol, one of her female friends. John left the Grafton Rooms and outside on West Derby Road, he watched as Judy and Carol climbed into a cab which took them towards the city centre. John flagged down another black cab and said to the driver, 'I'm not drunk and I'm not joking, but could you follow that taxi?'

'Played,' said the cabby.

'What, mate?' said John, closing the vehicle's door behind him.

'Well played, mate,' said the young taxi driver, 'I've always wanted someone to say "follow that taxi!"' And he tore off down West Derby Road. As the cab sped down Brunswick Road, the cabby said, 'Do you want me to hold back a bit, so they don't know they're being followed, or should I get in a bit closer?'

'Whatever you want, just don't lose them!'

'Don't worry, mate, they won't lose me,' the cabby reassured him, as he wove in and out of the traffic, closely tailing the other cab. The chase continued down Islington and stopped at Fraser Street, where the taxi stopped outside Mr Pickwicks club. 'Here y'are, just here'll do, mate,' John told the cabdriver, and handed him a good tip. He then went into the club, keeping an eye on his wife without being seen, but his friend McCardle saw him and shouted, 'Alright, John lad!' immediately blowing his cover.

Judy was furious, and stormed out of the club. For two days she refused to speak to him, but they eventually made up and Judy said she'd only been going out with her mates because they were around her age group, but John was unconvinced, as Carol was his age. A few days later Judy started going out on her own again, and this time John decided to hire a private investigator. A friend told him to go to Scott's Detective Agency off Dale Street, run by a woman in her 60s, Zena Scott-Archer, a seasoned private eye. John went in search of this detective agency under an archway off Dale Street, and found a warren of gloomy old fashioned solicitors' offices and the like in a narrow passageway. Up some steep stairs, instead of Scott's Detective Agency, he found a grim-looking grass-green door with flaking paint, on whose frosted glass pane, in faded gold letters, was written: Quicksilver Investigations – Established 1972.

As John opened the door a waft of paraffin from a heater hit his nostrils. Inside a man in his fifties sat behind an old desk, with fairy cakes, a Cornish pasty and a tartan thermos flask set out in front of him. He was reading the racing pages with a rolled-up cigarette dangling from his mouth. A sleeping tabby cat lay curled up in the in-tray and the place stank of coffee and Golden Virgina. The detective, Peter Maguire, bore a strong resemblance to the comedian Tom O'Connor; same white hair, same likeable face.

John Lofthouse confided his suspicions regarding his wife, and was told he'd need a recent photograph of her. This he duly received. John paid £100 up front, a lot of money in 1984, on top of Maguire's £30 a day fee plus expenses. John paid these rates without question, because he needed to know who his wife was seeing. Maguire was brilliant at disguises, and he followed Judy Lofthouse to a place called Flintlocks one night, and stood beside her as she flirted with two men in their early thirties. He learned that their first names were Jim and Roland. Then Maguire dropped a bombshell. He told John that his wife was seeing both of these men at the same time. He had actually watched them seriously kissing Judy in a very dark and secluded alleyway off Dale Street called Sweeting Street, at 2.30 in the morning, after the three of them had left a club. John was devastated; one man was bad enough, but this was too much to take in. John said he knew someone who had a shotgun, and he'd have no problem blasting the pair to kingdom come, but Maguire calmed him down and said he'd soon have the full names and addresses of the two men so they could be named in any adultery case.

A week went by, and Judy went to town on her own, and Macguire watched everything. He tailed her and the two men to a certain hotel on Mount Pleasant, outside which he waited all night in his car. Early in the morning, Roland walked out of the hotel and headed down Roscoe Street. Maguire followed him, and suddenly, the young man started singing the old Eddie Fisher song *I'm Walking Behind You* – as if he knew he was being followed, then suddenly turned around and ran back towards Mount Pleasant, where he seemed to go to ground pretty quickly. The private eye asked an old man on Rodney Street if he had seen a man pass by, but he hadn't. This happened twice more. Judy Lofthouse's two lovers would always vanish and it baffled Maguire.

Then something strange happened. One December morning at 2am, the two men left Pickwicks with Judy, kissed her, saw her to a taxi, then walked up Seymour Street, where Maguire followed them at a distance of about 30 yards. This time they weren't aware he was following them and they suddenly started singing a song that was out at that time by Jim Diamond called *I Should Have Known Better* (to lie to one as beautiful as you). As they sang Maguire closed in on them. Halfway up Russell Street, the men looked at each other, stopped singing, then started up again with the old Matt Monroe song *Charade*. Maguire stopped and lit a cigarette, then continued to follow the two men as they crossed over Mount Pleasant and walked down Rodney Street. As the men passed under one of the old fashioned lamp-posts, Maguire couldn't believe his eyes. The men's hair was getting paler by the second – going grey, in fact. By now Maguire was only twelve feet away and he heard one man to say to the other, 'Youth really *is* wasted on the young isn't it?'

His companion, who was now virtually bald and stooped, replied in a quavering voice, 'Yes, James, it is.'

Maguire gasped loudly in amazement and the two now old men

heard him and turned round. They seemed to recognise him and he sensed there was something truly uncanny about them, so he backed away with the men still standing there, looking at him.

Maguire told his client, John Lofthouse, what he had witnessed, and he couldn't believe him, but when John was later reconciled with his wife, she told him she had never seen the two young men after the night of the Rodney Street incident, and also confessed to having been under some kind of hypnotic spell when she was with them.

Encounter in a Cemetery

The following story took place in March 1963, and began, innocently enough, in a Cousins cake shop that once stood on the corner of Aigburth Road and Dalmeny Street. Two pretty Aigburth girls, Julie and Suzy, both aged 17, were gazing at a four-tier wedding cake in the shop window. It was decorated with white icing, pillars, strawberry-flavoured candy roses and so on, and on the top the bride and groom stood side by side, enclosed by a red heart-shaped floral frame. Suzy and Julie were dreaming away, each imagining it was their wedding cake, when a heavy hand landed on each of their shoulders. They turned, startled, and there was Cliff Adams, the most handsome lad they knew. He hailed from Wavertree, but got around on his scooter, and had female admirers across Liverpool. 'Hiya, Cliff,' both girls giggled in unison.

'Now wait, don't tell me,' said Cliff, 'you're Julie and you're Suzy. I never forget a bird's name, specially a lovely-looking bird.'

And then, to Julie, who was the blonde one, Cliff said, 'What have you done to your eyes, girl? They look dead lovely.'

Julie went red and said, 'They're falsies,' and starting giggling as she turned to look back in Cousins window.

'She means false eyelashes,' explained Suzy.

Cliff smiled and said to Julie, 'Don't be ashamed of looking lovely, girl.'

Suzy blushed when Cliff turned his attention to her saying,

'You're the brassy one aren't you?'

Suzy's was stuck for words. Cliff turned and pointed at his friend Keith Williams and said to Suzy, 'See him there? His name's Keith. He fancies you, don't you, Keith?'

Keith was still sitting on his scooter, and he nodded impatiently at his friend, then swore and said, 'Never mind them birds ... go and get us a sandwich cake. I'm famished.'

Cliff said to the girls 'Wait there a mo,' and went into Cousins. When he came out, Keith was chatting up the girls, and Julie was even sitting on his scooter as he showed her the controls and held his hand over hers as it clasped the throttle. 'It's like unsqueezing a lemon when you move off,' he was saying.

'Hey Keith here's your sandwich cake,' Cliff said, and when Keith turned, Cliff took his penknife out, cut the string round the box, took out the cake and tried to slam it in Keith's face, but instead caught Julie in the face. The cream, jam and sponge went everywhere and Suzy tried to help her clean up the mess.

'What d'you do that for you stupid bastard?' said Keith.

Cliff ignored him and clumsily tried to wipe the cream off Julie's face, but she pushed him away, saying to Suzy, 'Are my eyelashes still on?'

'Ah, Julie I'm sorry, love,' Cliff said, 'I was trying to hit Keith 'cos he swore in front of you and Suzy before. It really upset me. I'm really sorry, girl.'

'Get away from me, you stupid gawp,' snapped Julie.

Keith went back into the shop as Julie cooled down and came out a few minutes later with Cornish pasties and another sandwich cake, and pretended he was going to throw it at Cliff, but they all saw the funny side eventually, and Cliff took Julie into the chemist next door and explained what had happened to the woman behind the counter who let Julie use the staff toilet to clean herself up. Then the two lads took the girls for a spin on their scooters, and the sun came out. The foursome had a great day out, and visited a few cafes and pubs until they reached Widnes, where Keith had relatives, returning to Aigburth in the evening. Cliff asked Julie if he could see her again on

Thursday and she said yes, but Keith didn't seem that interested in Suzy, and she wasn't keen on him – she preferred Cliff. After the lads had gone, Julie told her friend a secret. She didn't actually like Cliff – she liked Keith. True, he wasn't as handsome, but he had a great personality, all of which was music to Suzy's ears.

On Thursday evening, Cliff and Keith met up with the girls on Aigburth Road, and took them to the Flying Saucer. Once inside, Cliff said to Julie, 'Do you like me?' and she nodded. Suzy looked at her, wondering if she'd tell the truth. Cliff said, 'Okay, I'm going to ask you to prove it. I went to visit my brother's grave in the cemetery yesterday, and I accidentally left my crash helmet behind. Would you go in that cemetery tonight and get it for me?'

'No, course I wouldn't.'

'Why not? You *do* like me don't you?'

'And if you liked me you wouldn't ask me to put my life in danger by going into a cemetery for some stupid helmet.'

'It isn't just any helmet, it was my brother's. Someone might have picked it up by now, but would you go and see if it's still there?'

'I'd go, Cliff,' Suzy put in, blushing slightly.

'Yeah, but I'm not asking you, am I?' said Cliff.

'Oh go and get it yourself,' Julie told him, and he seemed stunned. No girl had ever talked to him like that before. Thinking he'd make Julie jealous, Cliff took Suzy on his scooter to Allerton Cemetery – straight from the pub, and Keith followed on his scooter, with Julie riding pillion. Keith and Julie tried to talk Suzy out of going into the cemetery on her own, but Cliff kissed her and gave her clear directions on how to find the gravestone: near a certain tree by a bench in the middle of the cemetery. Suzy climbed over the low wall and by the light of the moon, headed for the centre of the cemetery. The minutes dragged on during which Cliff had a fight with Keith because he had kissed Julie. Meanwhile, Julie thought she heard a child's scream from inside the cemetery. A policeman came upon the scene and broke the fight up. Julie told him about her friend's idiotic search for a crash helmet in the cemetery, and the child's scream she had heard, and Cliff Adams said there was no lost helmet in there;

he'd just made it up. The policeman climbed over the cemetery wall and was gone for ages. He came back about 15 minutes later and went to a telephone box to call for an ambulance and backup. He'd found Suzy lying unconscious with a head injury in the middle of the cemetery. She was taken to hospital and treated for concussion. When she regained consciousness, she told a weird story. She had been looking for the crash helmet when she saw what she thought was a dog's head, peeping over a gravestone. As she got nearer, she realised it was the head of a teddy bear, and someone behind the gravestone was moving it up and down like a puppet. Then she heard a childish giggle, and saw the top of a boy's head over the gravestone. The boy had a large head of blonde hair and Suzy asked: 'What're you doing messing about in here at this time of night?'

The boy stood up. Below his full head of hair was the face of a skull, and below his neck he wore a white garment, like a burial shroud. He ran from the gravestone screaming with his arms in the air, and in one hand he held an old dirty-looking teddy bear.

Suzy's legs went to jelly and she collapsed, banging the side of her head against a grave marker. She lay there in shock and saw the ghastly-looking ghost of the child standing over her. 'If you die now, you can be my friend,' it pleaded.

Every so often, I still get reports of the child with the skull-like face who walks around Allerton Cemetery. I believe he died in the 1930s at the age of nine, and was buried with his beloved teddy bear.

WARNING FROM THE FUTURE

One afternoon, about 4pm, in December 1983, 39-year-old Ben Feeney was sitting in the Jolly Baker cafe, which used to be on the corner of Williamson Square. He was sitting drinking a coffee with a Cornish pasty in front of him and a copy of the *New Musical Express* in his hands, when in walked Michelle, a girl who Ben had dated for a while. They got talking and Michelle said she had been shopping, and was just having a break before getting the bus home. As they talked, a bald man in his sixties, or perhaps even older, came into the Jolly Baker on crutches without ordering anything and fixed each of them in turn with a peculiar look.

Ben had no respect for older people at that time in his life, and started to skit the man's appearance: his pale face with dark bags under the eyes and his cumbersome hearing aid with wires to both ears. He was dressed in a grey coat and tracksuit bottoms. Michelle felt uneasy but Ben told her to ignore him. He made jokes about the man, and in the end he said to him, 'You okay there, mate?' He sniggered and looked at Michelle for approval, but she kicked him under the table and told him to stop it. Ben looked back at the man – but he was gone. Surely he couldn't have moved away that fast on his crutches. This would have just been one of those unremarkable mysteries some of us encounter from time to time, and Ben forgot about the incident, but something bizarre was yet to happen.

It was in WH Smith, seven years later, that Ben bent down to pick up a book from a bottom shelf, and first heard a grating sound coming from his knees. Whenever he bent his legs, he could hear his knee joints scraping in their sockets. It was so noticeable that he mentioned it to his uncle, who said it sounded like arthritis. Ben went to his GP, and was referred to a specialist – who eventually told him he had a rare progressive osteopathic disorder which would leave him with crumbling chalk-like bones. Eventually, Ben had to use crutches because of this insidious condition. Then, in 1995, he started to get strange heart palpitations that would last for days on end. He cut out tea, coffee and soft drinks containing caffeine, but the palpitations continued. His doctor referred him to a cardiologist who dropped a bombshell – Ben had a grossly enlarged heart, which was likely to fail at any time. He stopped smoking and was put on daily medication. Around this time, Ben began to notice that his hair was clogging up the plughole whenever he showered, and eventually had to accept that he was going bald.

In December 2007, 63-year-old Ben hobbled into Sayers cafe on Williamson Square on crutches after struggling round the shops. He was out of breath, and felt and looked quite ill. Suddenly he recognised a familiar couple at one of the tables. A couple who were the image of a younger Ben Feeney and his former girlfriend Michelle, only she looked about 30. He stared at the couple and realised that the man was making fun of him, but curiosity got the better of him, and so he moved closer to the table, at which the young man asked, 'You okay there, mate?'

At that moment, Ben felt an overwhelming sense of *déjà vu*, and remembered how he had sat in that same cafe when it was called the Jolly Baker, 24 years before, in 1983, and only then did he realise that he had somehow seen himself as he would appear in the future. But when Ben looked really closely at the couple, he saw that they now no longer bore any resemblance to a young Ben and Michelle, which deepened the mystery. Ben was wearing his Apple iPod at the time when this strange incident occurred, and he wondered if it had looked like an oversized hearing aid to the Ben Feeney of 1983. Another local mystery of space and time – or perhaps just a coincidence?

The Haunted Ring

On 9 April 1967, Madame Borel de Bitche, the owner of the famous Grand National horse Kilburn, had £4000 worth of jewellery stolen from her first-floor suite at the Adelphi Hotel. The thief had slipped into her suite and knew exactly where the jewels were kept – in the dressing table drawer. As far as I know, the thief was never caught, but there were rumours that the stolen jewellery was seemingly cursed, and receivers and fences who handled it died, became seriously ill, or lost family members. The jewellery stolen included a square blue diamond solitaire ring, worth a thousand pounds in 1967, earrings, a bee-shaped brooch and a pearl necklace. These pearls were said to have had a dark history of tragedy attached to them. There is an old superstition, going back to Biblical times, regarding pearls, that they always bring sadness. The only person for whom the jewellery had not been unlucky was Madame de Bitche.

Also at the Adelphi, going a little further back in time to the

1950s, there was another jewellery theft. A man named Richard Miller left the Adelphi one windy March evening in 1958 and set off to see Buddy Holly and the Crickets at the Philharmonic Hall. When he returned, he discovered that some money was missing from his suitcase, together with a box containing an old pigeon-blood-red ruby ring that had been passed down from Miller's great grandmother. It was later revealed that a man of middle height with a distinctive mole between his eyebrows, had been seen hurrying down the corridor outside Miller's room on the evening of the theft.

The thief, George, spent the stolen money on ale at the Midland pub (facing Central Station), then set off for the Cavern. That night he met the most beautiful woman he had ever set eyes on in all his 30-odd years. Her name was Carol, and George started dating her. She told him he was a dead ringer for Tommy Steele, and that won him over completely and he decided to give her the stolen ruby ring, telling her it was a family heirloom. Carol fell for this patter, looking upon it as an engagement ring, and she began to flash it off to all her workmates in Woolworths. Then strange things began to happen.

One grey afternoon, George and Carol were in the Kardomah Cafe on Bold Street, and as George got up to go to the toilet, a foreign-looking woman left her table and came over to Carol and told her to get rid of the ring because there was a dark aura around it. Carol was affronted and said it had belonged to her fiancés great-grandmother, but the dark-haired woman shook her head and said, 'No, love. He's lied to you. Please get rid of that ruby, or you'll be dead and buried by the autumn.'

The woman left and when George returned he found Carol in floods of tears. She told him what the woman had said and George went to look for her, but a waitress grabbed his arm and told him that she was a gypsy who told fortunes at a kiosk on Bold Street. She warned him not to argue with her because she had cursed people in the past. George dismissed the whole thing as utter nonsense, and took Carol to a cinema on Lime Street to see the Norman Wisdom picture *One Good Turn*. Halfway through the film Carol happened to glance down at something on her hand that was catching her eye.

Something was moving on the ruby. She made out the face of an old woman, faintly lit up in the ruby, shaking her head in a very disapproving way, and she let out a shriek. The man sitting in front of her turned round hushing her to be quiet. 'Do you mind? I'm trying to watch a film here!' George too could see the face. Carol yanked the ring off her finger, then handed it back to him saying, 'I don't want it anymore', then hurried out of the cinema. George ran after her and took her to the Beehive pub, promising that he'd thrown the ring away and she believed him.

That night Carol stayed with George at his flat in Lawrence Gardens, a tenement off Scotland Road. At four in the morning, she got up to go to the toilet, and noticed a faint red glow coming from the partially closed drawer of the bedside cabinet. When she opened it she saw that it was coming from that accursed ruby ring and now projected an image of a huge grinning skull on to the ceiling. Carol screamed the place down, and turned the light on. She quickly got dressed, then stormed out, this time leaving George for good.

George kept the ring for a few days more, and suffered a succession of terrible mishaps and accidents, as did everyone in his family. He decided to give the ring back. He sneaked back into the Adelphi, distracted the hotel receptionist, and then left the ring in an envelope with an anonymous note behind the counter. Mr Miller was due to book out of the hotel that day, and was overjoyed to get the ring back.

Another You

The *Titanic* missed that iceberg in 1912 and arrived in New York in record time, but was torpedoed by a U boat in 1915 when the liner was used as a United States troopship, and, in 1963, John F Kennedy decided to obey his grim hunch whilst visiting Dallas by having a Perspex bullet-proof bubble fitted over the Presidential car – thus surviving two simultaneous assassination attempts in Dealey Plaza. Unfortunately, people in higher power than JFK put a bomb on Air Force One, killing the President and his wife on the flight back to Washington DC, and, in December 1980, Mark Chapman's gun jammed ...

In the light of new findings in Quantum Physics, all of the above-mentioned events took place, because it would seem we are living in a topsy-turvy universe of countless parallel worlds, and even you, reader, take on a million roles in those different worlds. One version of you may be sitting reading this book right now, while another version of you exists – only your sex may be different – and you may be sitting in this parallel world reading a German copy of this book because Hitler decided to conquer Britain instead of attacking Russia, and the Nazi Party – in this alternate strand of existence – managed to develop atomic fission before the United States, and launched a series of A-Bomb attacks on New York and Moscow with their long-range V2 rockets ... What if, under some circumstances presently unknown to science, one of the countless other versions of you came into this 'channel' of reality?

I believe this occasionally happens. In 1975, Carl, a quiet and inoffensive 13-year-old, was seized by the scruff of his collar one evening as he played football in the Botanic Park off Edge Lane. A middle-aged man, Mr Williams, literally collared Carl because he swore the boy had just smashed the bay window of his living room. Seven witnesses saw Carl throw the stone through the window, but Carl swore it wasn't him, and he managed to free himself from the grip of the irate house-holder and ran home. Days later, Carl called at his girlfriend Dawn's flat, in Sidney Gardens, only to have the door slammed in his face as she called him a two-timing rat. Dawn and her friends had seen Carl kissing a girl named Rosie by the Steble Fountain in town that morning – even though Carl was actually miles away watching telly in his home in Winifred Street at the time. Carl confronted Rosie over the supposed kissing incident, and she spat at him, because she claimed he was now seeing a girl from Huyton.

Carl finally realised that something very strange was going on when his mother claimed he had almost hit her whilst riding his Chopper bike ten minutes before. Carl's Chopper had a puncture, but his mother couldn't believe it wasn't him. And, then on the following Saturday, Carl actually came face to face with his doppelganger in Lodge Lane Baths. He had swum two lengths when someone seized his feet and pulled him under. Carl kicked violently, freeing himself then surfaced gasping. He swam to the side of the pool, pursued by the psychopathic swimmer – and saw to his horror, that the pursuer was his exact double. Carl's friends heard his cries for help, and when they saw the 'other Carl' they took him to be some relative at first, but the deadly double quickly dived to the bottom of the pool – and never resurfaced. He was never seen again.

An Angel on Mount Pleasant

Snow-filled marbled clouds hung oppressively low over Liverpool that Christmas Eve in 1965 when 20-year-old Bill Hadley sat close to the hissing blue and white jets of the gas fire at his girlfriend's condemned house on Cambridge Street in the city centre. He watched *Stingray* on the black and white telly. Millicent Kirkpatrick, his 19-year-old fiancée, had finished twisting the yards of coloured crepe paper into decorations that her younger sister Nell was tacking to the ceiling, atop a rickety step ladder. The living room and hall of the draughty old house were festooned with coloured balloons, concertina-folded orange and indigo bells and rainbow paper chains. The Christmas tree was coiled in silver and gold tinsel, topped with an old fairy doll. 'You're going to get corned-beef legs sitting that close to the fire, Millie,' Millicent's mother, Joan, warned her, as she sipped tea from a cup with a missing handle, taking a break from writing Christmas cards. Millicent sat reading the song listings on *Rubber Soul*, the brand new Beatles album Bill had bought her. The couple were due to go to a party at a friend's flat in Gerard Gardens, but Joan had insisted on treating her daughter and future son-in-law to a roast dinner first.

After dinner Bill was enjoying a small hot toddy of whisky when he noticed Millie gazing out into the wintry street. She was watching a shabbily dressed man of about 30 who was sitting on an old packing case, eating something, and sharing his meagre meal with a little mongrel dog. Fine snow was falling, whipped into whirling eddies by the sharp December wind. There wasn't another soul about outside as the big freeze began, and Millicent took some food outside to the poor vagrant, even though her mother and Bill warned her not to. Millie proffered a plate of roast dinner and a couple of mince pies in a tissue. 'Thank you so much,' the stranger said, his eyes full of appreciation.

'Millie!' Bill shouted from across the street, 'Come on! Leave him! We've got to get going soon!'

Mrs Kirkpatrick shook her head as she peered over Bill's shoulder at her daughter. About ten minutes went by, and Billy marched out of the house to fetch his sweetheart, but he found her standing in the splintering-cold street with just the little dog at her feet. The tramp had gone. Millie had a strange far-away look in her eyes, and when she went back into the house, she called for her 14-year-old sister Nell, and then talked to her in hushed tones. Nell seemed intrigued by whatever Millie was telling her, and Bill watched with a quizzical face as the sisters left the room and went up to Millie's bedroom. 'What's going on?' Bill asked Millie's mum, who replied, 'She can be deep as the ocean sometimes that girl.' Joan then glanced at the clock and said: 'You're going to be late for that party; go up and tell her to get a move on.'

Bill went upstairs and halted at Millie's bedroom door. He was about to knock when he heard the low voices of the sisters – saying some prayer. 'Amen,' they said simultaneously, and Bill rapped on the door. Minutes later, when the couple left for the party, Bill asked why she and Nell had been praying. 'You wouldn't believe me,' was Millie's reply, and Bill said, 'Try me.'

'That tramp was an angel.' Bill returned a bemused gaze. 'He told me he had been left to roam the world as a down-and-out for years because he doubted and disobeyed God, and as a result a little girl almost died. He asked me to pray for him, to ask God to forgive him.'

'And why would this "angel" ask you in particular?' Bill asked, with a sneer.

'I was the girl who was almost killed,' came the shock reply. 'When I was five, I got stuck up a tree in Abercromby Park. I slipped and hung on to a branch over some railings. I closed my eyes as I lost my grip, and I remember a pair of hands holding my waist, and something lowering me down on to the pavement. I ran off in shock and was hit by a car. I was in hospital for a month, and almost died twice. The angel told me that had I fallen from the tree, I wouldn't have hit the railings. God had assured him of that, but the angel intervened because he thought I'd be impaled.'

As the couple turned the corner, they both saw the vagrant by Notre Dame Convent on Mount Pleasant, sitting on his old suitcase with his head bowed. 'I prayed for you,' Millie whispered, and he said a soft 'Thank you.' All of a sudden, a beam of light shone down from the darkening sky, singling out the stranger. He looked skywards, and was transformed into a figure in white and gold garments with long coppery hair. He smiled, and spoke unintelligible words, perhaps Enochian, the language of the angels. And then he was gone, and a peaceful silence descended on Mount Pleasant.

ANGELS OVER LIVERPOOL

Barbara, a Liverpool woman in her late fifties, was about to end it all. She had lost her husband to cancer after 30 years of marriage, and now her only child, 27-year-old Angela, hadn't spoken to her in weeks after of a silly argument. On top of that, Barbara's two sisters had also fallen out with her because Barbara had asked them to help look after their 84-year-old mother, who was suffering from senile dementia. Now Barbara had been forced to place her mother in a home, and was racked with guilt as a result. Barbara looked at a bottle of powerful painkillers that had been prescribed to her late husband, and decided to swallow them all. Her gaze then turned to the beautifully-kept garden outside her West Derby home – the one place that she had looked upon as her sanctum. The roses were budding, but Barbara thought she'd never see them in bloom. As she surveyed the green haven she had tended to so lovingly for decades, something strange took place. The sliding door leading to the garden started to slowly open, startling her. The sun came out and bathed the garden in its warm golden light, and the scent of lavender drifted into the room. Barbara had no belief in the paranormal, and had never been a spiritual person. She was a grounded, down-to-earth no nonsense soul, but she suddenly felt as if something had entered the living room, and yet, she was not afraid, which surprised her.

As she walked towards the sliding door which had opened of its own accord, Barbara felt what she could only describe as 'two loving arms' wrap themselves around her. She felt they were the strong but gentle arms of a man, and she slowly sat on the sofa in this strange embrace, and began to sob. As she closed her eyes, she was amazed to find herself sitting on her father's lap the way she used to as a child. She felt so loved and safe that she was afraid to open her eyes in case the embrace faded away, but a kind voice in her mind told her that her father was 'somewhere near' and when she asked who she was talking to, the voice told her that he was an angel, come to look after her for a while.

When Barbara opened her eyes, she felt as if this 'angel' was still in the room, and she went to throw the bottle of painkillers out – but they had gone, disappeared, never to be seen again. Her entire outlook changed for the better after the incident, and she has since remarried. Barbara believes an angel intervened in her life that day in 2009, and she isn't alone in her experiences, for there seems to be a divine invasion across the world, as more of these angelic encounters are reported, and the north west of England is no exception to this phenomenon.

In 2010, 22-year-old Liverpool John Moores student Sophie started seeing fellow student Jack, and after a brief courtship she became pregnant and moved in with Jack at his parent's London home. Sophie was a very spiritual girl who believed in angels, whereas Jack was a complete sceptic, and they always had heated discussions whenever the subject of the supernatural arose. Sophie maintained that her grandmother, who had died when she was eleven, now visited her as an angel, but Jack thought this was ridiculous. However, in December 2010, something took place which converted him from a hard-boiled sceptic to a devout believer. A scan of Sophie's baby confirmed that it was 'the wrong way round' – breeched. It would be born feet-first instead of head-first. Attempts were made by a qualified midwife to rotate the baby by manipulating the mother's abdomen, but the birth proved very difficult, and Sophie suddenly went into cardiac arrest. She stopped breathing and her heart ceased beating. The baby girl had to be delivered by Caesarean section, and after delivery, she too stopped breathing because the umbilical cord had become compressed, cutting off her oxygen supply. Sophie died for almost two minutes, and Jack wept, because he felt his world had just ended; he had lost his partner and his daughter. Jack recalled the stories Sophie had told him about her 'angel Nan' and so he openly prayed for her to intervene, as a surgeon and three nurses escorted him from the ward.

Jack slumped into a seat in the corridor in tears. When he looked up a minute later, a silver-haired woman was smiling at him through the window of the door leading to the maternity ward. Then the woman's face vanished before his eyes. Seconds later the door burst open, and a nurse told Jack that his wife had been resuscitated and the baby had started breathing again.

Mother and daughter made a full recovery, and when the couple visited Sophie's parents at their Mossley Hill Home, Jack was flabbergasted by a framed photograph of Sophie's Nan on the sideboard, because it was the face of the grey-haired lady who had smiled at him through the window as he sat in despair in the hospital corridor. Sophie recalled her Nan visiting her in a black void when she had physically died during childbirth. She had told her it wasn't her time to pass over, and that she'd have to go back for the sake of the baby and Jack, and she had held Sophie's hand and pulled her down a long tunnel leading to daylight. Sophie says that her Nan still visits in times of trouble, and that she returned from the life beyond to become an angel who guides and protects herself and her family. On many occasions, Sophie, Jack and other people have found white feathers – traditionally said to be signs of angel visitation – all over the house.

In March 2011, a man we shall call Carl, coming to the end of a long sentence in Walton Gaol, wrote to tell me how he was visited by an angel in the dead of night in his cell after receiving a Dear John letter from his wife. She could not wait for him to be released any more, as she wanted to have children and settle down, and now she had met someone. Carl felt depressed and suicidal because he worshipped his wife and wrote to her regularly. He awoke on his bunk at four in the morning, fighting back tears, because he had just had a vivid dream that he was a free man, walking down Church Street with his wife. He did something he'd never done before in his life, he said a prayer. Over and over he begged God to make his wife change her mind and come back to him, and after the prayer, a sweet scent infiltrated the cell. He and his cellmate both smelt it and heard a voice say, 'He heard your prayer.'

Three days later, Carl's wife wrote to him, saying she loved him and would wait another year until he was released. That day Carl found a large white feather on his bed. When his wife visited him a few days later, she told him a strange thing. She had also found a large white feather lying on her bed the same night as Carl found his.

In October 2010, 74-year-old Margaret from Anfield fell ill with suspected Swine Flu, and lay shivering in bed. At around 9pm she became very weak, and fearing she was about to die, started to pray. All of a sudden, the ceiling seemed to open to reveal a vast golden tunnel lined with winged angels, and a powerful white light shone down the tunnel, lighting up the bedroom. A woman in a white robe emerged from the tunnel and hovered over the bed. It was Margaret's friend Jean, from Clitheroe. Jean told Margaret to rest, and she would be okay. Margaret lost consciousness at this point, and woke eight hours later, feeling hungry. Margaret's daughter Elaine had heard strange music coming from the bedroom and had seen a light shining under the door but when she went in, all she saw was her mum sleeping. Three days later, Margaret heard that her friend in Clitheroe had just passed away from pneumonia – on the very night Margaret had seen her in the tunnel of angels.

The *Liverpool Echo* ran a two-page spread on my investigation into local cases of Angels in May 2011, and I was inundated with fascinating letters from readers detailing their own experiences with angels and the white-feather phenomenon. The following three are typical of the letters I received:

Dear Tom,

I was very intrigued to read about the white feathers mentioned in your article about angels in the Liverpool Echo as I have had a number of these experiences in the past. On one occasion when I was eleven, my father was seriously ill in hospital, and I recall lying in bed, hearing my mother crying in the next room, and so I said a prayer, then fell into an uneasy sleep. I dreamt a tall man in a white robe was standing at the foot of my bed, and he told me he was an angel, and that my father would get well soon. In the dream, he said he'd give me a sign. I woke up around 4am, and moonlight was streaming through the window, and there, on the duvet, was a white feather. The next morning the hospital called to say my father had made a sudden recovery. When my wife was desperately ill in hospital a few years ago, I was allowed to sleep in a special room at the hospital, and had the same dream featuring the same angel, and once again he said he'd give me a sign so I'd know all would be well. That morning at 8am a nurse came into the room to wake me and drew my attention to a white feather on the end of my bed. My wife was sitting up and laughing in her sickbed by noon. I can't explain these incidents, but similar ones are happening all the time.

Alan Burgess
Liverpool 14

The second letter, from Rita James, mentions a very dramatic case of divine intervention ...

Hi

I read your accounts of local reports of angelic beings recently in the Echo, and the stories reminded me of a strange incident which took place in my youth. In July 1962 I was given a lift up to Southport to see the Beatles at the Cambridge Hall (now the Southport Arts Centre), and also saw Joe Brown and his band, the Bruvvers, play there. I think Gerry and the Pacemakers were also at that gig, and afterwards I managed to get autographs from the Fab Four, and also had a chat with Joe Brown. As I left the venue on Lord Street, I heard a car horn and a screech, and in a split second, I realised I was about to be knocked down. Something lifted me up off the roadway and carried me about ten feet, where I came down to the pavement with a gentle bump. I recall a few people, including Joe Brown, gasping, and a policeman who had witnessed this weird happening said, 'How did you do that?'

To this day I have no idea what lifted me out of the way of that car, but in the light of the accounts in your article, I would say it might have been a real-life guardian angel of some sort.

Sincerely,
Mrs Rita James
Liverpool 19

Brian Noakes of Wallasey recalled a mysterious life-saving gesture by a possible angelic being during his Norris Green childhood:

Tom,

I am writing to say how much I enjoyed your stories about local angel incidents and would like to add my own into the mix. In 1966, when I was just six years of age, I decided to climb on to the back of an ice cream van one afternoon outside my home on Utting Avenue East, Norris Green. The ice cream van drove off and picked up a bit of speed, and I was too scared to let go. I clung on in a state of absolute terror and began to cry. As the van sped up Storrington Avenue, I felt someone lift me off the vehicle and put me down gently on the pavement. When I looked around, there was no one there, and being lost I ran to a woman and told her what I had done and that I was lost. The woman told me off, saying I shouldn't have hung on to the back of the ice cream van, and she led me home, all the way to my door. I told my mother what had happened and she said it had been an angel. I can still remember this strange incident as if it had happened yesterday.

Bedside Visit at the Royal

A few years ago a couple in their late seventies we shall call Geoff and Eileen were both admitted to the Royal Hospital in Liverpool. They had been married for 50 years. Geoff was admitted with heart trouble, and Eileen because she had been suffering from a long illness and wasn't expected to live long. Eileen was in a bed in the women's section of the hospital and Geoff was in the male section. About a fortnight after being admitted, Eileen passed away, and her family decided they wouldn't tell Geoff, in case the shock affected his health, but on the afternoon Eileen died Geoff was very surprised to see Eileen sitting on the edge of his bed. He thought he was hallucinating at first so he asked a fellow patient, 'Can you see a lady sitting on my bed?'

And Eileen smiled, then said to this patient in the next bed, 'Can you?' and laughed. The patient, a man named Paul, said he could. Eileen told Geoff she was better now, and he hugged her and asked how this was possible. She told him to rest, and to stop worrying about her. A nurse came in and reminded Geoff he was being seen by a consultant in 15 minutes. The nurse also saw Eileen and smiled at her and exchanged niceties. When the nurse went back out, a woman, dressed in a long black dress, from the Victorian or Edwardian era, entered the ward and stood silently at Eileen's side. She was also wearing an outdated bonnet of some sort and her face was deathly pale. This strange visitor was seen by a porter, and Paul, who initially thought she was a goth. He estimated her age to be about 25. Eileen kissed and hugged Geoff and said she'd see him again in a few days and told him once again to 'Worry over nothing, everything will be okay, Geoff, I promise you.' Eileen then left, escorted by the stranger, and the nurse watched them go. In fact Eileen's arm brushed against her elbow.

Geoff's grief-stricken daughters and son-in-law came in to visit later that day, and Geoff told them he'd seen their mother earlier on, and that she had made a miraculous recovery. At this time, Eileen was in the morgue, so the children and son-in-law assumed he had either dreamt of the visitation or been visited by someone who looked like Eileen. But Paul confirmed the story, and so did the porter and the nurse. Each of them described Eileen's pale blue satin jacket and skirt, and the butterfly brooch in her lapel. Eileen had such an outfit in her wardrobe and just such a brooch. Geoff's daughter brought in five photographs of her aunties and a picture of Eileen, and straight away, Paul and the nurse correctly identified Eileen from the selection of photographs. On the following day, Geoff passed away with a smile on his face after calling out his wife's name.

A retired doctor who has worked at the Royal, said that he had heard of similar cases before, and was intrigued to hear of the woman in Victorian clothes, because she has been seen regularly by staff and visitors over the years, and some mediums who have looked into this case believe she is some sort of spirit guide, and all feel she is connected to the old Royal Infirmary on Pembroke Place, just across the road from the Royal Hospital on Prescot Road.

Gypsy Marie's Fatal Predictions

This is a rather short but nevertheless very strange true story. In January 1958, Marie, said to have been of Romany descent, set up a fortune-telling service on Bold Street, where the Petticoat Arcade is now situated. A sceptic from Liverpool University, a tutor in mathematics specialising in probability, visited Marie and tried to give her ten shillings. Marie refused the money, and told him that he had only come to try and catch her out. The tutor asked Marie for three definite incidents which would be happening in the near future. Marie looked into her crystal ball for a while, then told him he would be dead within six months. To prove her powers, she predicted a plane crash with a great loss of life that would take place locally in snow in a month's time. She could clearly see the three legged symbol of the Isle of Man. The sceptic grinned, 'Oh really? I must take extra care. And what's the second prediction?'

The gypsy said that there would be another plane crash on the banks of the Mersey, and a single man would die. This man would be known to a friend of his. Then, at the end of June, she predicted that he would literally drop dead. The lecturer then produced a small reel to reel tape recorder from a backpack and announced that he had captured these sham predictions. If they failed to come true, he would be sending the transcript of the recording to the *Daily Post* and *Echo*. He seemed pretty pleased with himself.

A month later, on 27 February 1958, 35 people died when their plane, a Bristol Wayfarer, owned by Silver City Airways, crashed into Winter Hill, in Lancashire. There were seven survivors, but rescuers had to fight their way through heavy snowdrifts to reach the scene of the crash. The plane had flown from the isle of Man. This made the university tutor a bit nervous, but he put it down to coincidence.

Then, on 30 March, a two-seater Tiger Moth crashed into the muddy banks of the River Mersey, killing its pilot, 38-year-old aircraft instructor Jack Green, of Queen's Drive, Liverpool. His 32-year-old pupil, Arthur Hobin, of Huyton, was rescued from the quicksand and rushing tide. The tail of the plane could be seen for hours sticking out of the sandbanks.

By now the lecturer was very unnerved, and fearing he just might drop dead, he gave the recording of the interview with Gypsy Marie to his friend, a man who worked as a journalist at the *Liverpool Daily Post* and *Echo*. In June of that year, the sceptical lecturer dropped dead whilst visiting his father in Cornwall. His heart was found to be perfect, and the coroner had to record a verdict of death by natural causes. Not long afterwards, Gypsy Marie vanished into obscurity.

Ho Tay

In the early 1980s, there was a well-kept cafe called the Boston Diner in Williamson Square, sandwiched between the Queen's Arms and R J Evans & Co, an estate agent's. One morning, 30-year-old Keith, from Wavertree, went into the Boston Diner for a full English breakfast, and an old friend of his, Jack Molyneux, came in too. Now, Keith had gone to school with Jack, and liked him, but Jack was a bit of a tea-leaf. On this morning, just as Keith was ready to have his breakfast, Jack turned up and asked if he wanted any Walkmans or Cabbage Patch dolls. Keith declined and ordered Jack a coffee. Jack Molyneux sat there with a face as long as Lime Street, then noticed a copy of the previous day's *Echo* and began to browse through it. He always read the last little item in the newspaper, a tiny square on the back page called 'The Finishing Touch', usually a saying or proverb. On this occasion it was: *An ounce of luck is worth a pound of wisdom.* This jogged Molyneux's memory, and he pulled an odd ornament out of his pocket and laid it next to Keith's plate. It was a little golden figure of a fat bald man with far-eastern features. He held a staff in his hands.

'That's a lucky Buddha. Worth a few bob that,' said Jack.

'Where d'you get it?'

'You're one person I wouldn't lie to,' said Molyneux.

'The only time I believe you is when you admit you're a liar; where did you knock it off?'

'In Chinatown,' Molyneux admitted, then pleaded for money. 'Give us a fiver – I'm brassic. I'm on my uppers, Keith.'

Keith picked the Buddha up. 'It's heavy.'

'Solid gold,' Jack assured him, 'I had it valued.'

'Shut up,' said Keith, taking a fiver from his wallet and sliding it across to Jack.

'Ah, cheers, Keith, you'll have luck, lad.' Then, after a last sip of his coffee he went straight to William Hill the bookmakers.

On his way home Keith pulled into the filling station, opposite the Mount Vernon pub. A man there saw the golden Buddha in the front window of Keith's car, and said, 'I won't have any luck now I've seen that.' Keith asked him what he meant. 'That's Ho Tay, a sixth century Buddhist monk. We had one. Three house fires, a suicide and a murder, all in eighteen months.'

'I don't believe in superstition, said Keith. 'Our Lord wouldn't allow all that. You make your own luck, mate.'

Anyway, Keith went home to his house in Wavertree Vale, and when his wife Kim saw the Buddha figure, she begged him to throw it out. 'Get shut of it, Keith,' she said, but Keith just grinned, and took his wife's glass swans off the mantelpiece and replaced them with the golden Buddha, saying, 'You idiot. If anything weird happens I'll kiss your mother's backside ... that's how sure I am this is all rubbish.'

The following night, Keith was coming back from the pub with his mate, when he saw something odd. On the curtains of his bay window, was projected the silhouette of a bald obese person doing Kung Fu type of movements, kicking his leg in the air and swinging a staff about. Keith was dumbfounded, suspecting his wife had got someone to play a practical joke on him. He entered the house to find the parlour light on, but no one about. Keith's wife was in bed with her rollers in, fast asleep. Keith searched the house from top to bottom to satisfy his curiosity, but there was no practical joker to be seen. He was so unnerved by the incident, he got rid of the Buddha by hiding it inside an old dilapidated grandfather clock, which he gave to a man he secretly couldn't stand named Brian Beglahn.

Some bizarre things later happened to Brian. The man's house was broken into one evening while he was out, and one of the burglars found himself confronted with a bald, bizarrely dressed man of Chinese appearance who thrashed him with a long stick, ramming the end of the staff into the burglar's eye, knocking him out. The other burglar fled, but was caught by the police. When they heard the house breakers' testimony, they searched Brian Beglahn's house for the little bald-headed martial artist to no avail. A year after this, Brian had his living room walls painted by a decorator named Geoff. When Brian paid him for the job, Geoff casually asked who 'the funny little fat Chinese man' was who kept peeping in at him from the hallway as he painted the living room.

Brian later found the figure of Ho Tay in the grandfather clock and sold it for £2.50 to a second-hand shop on Wavertree Road. The present whereabouts of the statue are unknown.

TELEPORTATIONS

Some readers may recall the television series *The Tomorrow People*, first broadcast in 1973, which featured a team of psychic teenagers who used their powers to fight evil and save the Earth. The Tomorrow People were the emerging specimens of Homo Superior (the successor to Homo Sapiens), the next stage of human evolutionary development, and were endowed with telepathy, telekinesis (the ability to move things by sheer willpower), and teleportation – the power to transport themselves across almost any distance in an instant. The Homo Superiors dubbed this teleportation talent 'jaunting', and, as unbelievable as it sounds, I experienced this once, but whether it was me doing the jaunting or some supernatural agency, I could not say. I was 13 at the time, and was at a friend's old Victorian house in Wavertree. He was at the top of a long flight of stairs, I was at the bottom, and his older brother was behind me. A moment later I was at the top of the stairs, and my friend said, 'How did you do that?' I was as baffled as him. His older brother said I vanished before his eyes, then reappeared at the top of the stairs.

In the late 1830s and early 1840s, Queen Victoria lived in mortal fear of meeting the first royal stalker in history: 14-year-old ragamuffin Edward Jones, who had the uncanny ability to enter Buckingham Palace at will. 'The Boy Jones' as the Press called him, was obsessed with the pretty 19-year-old queen, and made three well-reported visits to Victoria, but is thought to have somehow gained access to Buckingham Palace on many more occasions. On one occasion he stole the Queen's knickers from her dressing chamber, and one afternoon he sat on the royal throne, and even hid under her sofa. The Boy Jones also read the Queen's letters.

Officials of the early Secret Service and Home Office captured Jones and interrogated him, desperate to find out how he could enter Buckingham Palace so easily, but the grimy street urchin would just smile. Such a security issue would not arise again until 1982 when Michael Fagan sneaked into the palace to ask Her Majesty for 'a ciggy', but lovesick Boy Jones was somehow able to bypass the most elaborate security measures put in place. At the time, the authorities were trying their best to keep a scandal at the palace under wraps from republican radicals, and whatever this secret was, they were afraid of Jones discovering it. Some even feared that the pesky intruder would be paid by anarchists to shoot Victoria. After a secret trial, Edward Jones was escorted to Liverpool under lock and key, to be deported to Australia, but the boy was involved in a bureaucratic farce with the port authorities and was at liberty to roam Liverpool for weeks. Many in London and Liverpool believed the boy possessed supernatural powers which allowed him to enter locked houses, but no one ever discovered how he was able to repeatedly enter Buckingham Palace so effortlessly. Was he a teleporter? Jones was eventually deported to Australia, where he died, an alcoholic, in his late sixties after falling off a bridge.

Scientists have already successfully teleported photons and particles of matter, and are now looking at more complex molecules and viruses to beam across space, with a view to one day beaming humans from one place to another. Concorde crossed the Atlantic in three hours, but the time isn't far away when Mars will be reached in five minutes.

This is a strange and unexplained story of possible teleportation that dates back to 29 May 2009, the day before the FA cup final at Wembley. Two Liverpool men in their thirties, John Cunningham and Jimmy Powell, were both ardent Evertonians, and both had obtained tickets for Wembley to see their team play in the final against Chelsea, but being hard-up and out of work, the lads didn't have enough money for the train journey down to London, and had arranged to get a lift from their friend Frank Scott, who lived in

Helsby, just north of Chester. The lads had to get the train from Central Station, all the way over to Wirral and down the Wirral line through Ellesmere Port, where they rendezvoused with Frank in his dilapidated transit van. This van was in such a bad state that when Jimmy looked under the bonnet, there was a weed growing out of the filth that had accumulated between the chassis and the side of the engine. But beggars can't be choosers, and so the three men set off along the M56, bound for the M6.

John Cunningham, who knew all there was to know about superstitions, said there was no Junction 13 on the M56, and he's right of course. Junction 12 is to be found at Frodsham, and the next junction is 14, just after Helsby. Anyway, as the transit travelled along, the engine started making ominous noises, and by the time it reached Wolverhampton, it was steadily losing power, and Frank had to pull over. This was the day before the cup final, 29 May 2009. Jimmy Powell had a friend who ran a pub near Wembley and had everything gone to plan, the three lads would have stayed overnight at his pub, but now they were stranded on a deserted road surrounded by farmland in the accursed van. Frank wasn't a member of the AA or RAC and as usual, had not made any provision for a breakdown. Between them they had 60 pounds, so they went to the local pub and returned to the van around 11pm to get some sleep. By now, Jimmy, John and Frank had given up on Wembley.

At around three in the morning, Jimmy woke up and left the van to relieve himself. As he urinated against the back wheel of the van, he spotted something unusual – a standing stone about 20 feet away – a long dark megalith just like one of the ley stones at Stonehenge, which had probably been there for thousands of years. The stone was ablaze with a steady bright green light, as if someone was training a laser on it. Jimmy took in the eerie spectacle, but was so tired, he just staggered back into the van and was soon fast asleep again. Some time later, Jimmy couldn't say when, but it was still dark, the transit started to shake, and John Cunningham was woken by vibrations and loud humming. Eventually the sound subsided, and John and Jimmy drifted back off to sleep. The next morning, John was awakened by Frank shaking him violently.

'Alright, get off! What? What?' John said, grumpily, for he had a hangover from the night before and his head pounded with a throbbing pain centred over his left eye.

'Come outside, you won't believe it.'

John got to his feet and stepped down off the back of the van. This was definitely not Wolverhampton and there was another of those tall stones standing nearby. The three men walked off and covered over a mile before they came to a sign that read 'Dunkirk'.

'Oh my God!' said Jimmy Powell. 'We're in France!' He saw a stranger walking past, about a hundred feet away, and he went to him shouting, 'Excusez moi, monsieur!'

The man, who looked to be about 70, wore a flat cap, tweed jacket and brown trousers tucked into a pair of Wellington boots. Jimmy asked him if he spoke English, and the elderly stranger shot back a puzzled look. 'Well, why wouldn't I?' he replied in a Kentish accent, and walked off. The three lads eventually realised they were in Kent. They hadn't known there was a Dunkirk in Kent, just a few miles west of Canterbury – but the mystery of how they had travelled over 170 miles from Wolverhampton as they slept in a broken-down van could not be resolved, and probably never will be. Frank wondered if the transit had been towed down there, perhaps by mistake, but decided that was very unlikely.

The three men were able to hitch-hike to Wembley from Kent, and got to see the FA Cup Final, even though their beloved team was defeated by Chelsea. Back in Liverpool, John and Jimmy told everyone about the weird incident, and even contacted several newspapers, but unsurprisingly, no one believed them. There is an another intriguing possibility: that something teleported the van and its three occupants across England in the small hours of that May morning in 2009. Teleportation is the transportation of a person or object from one place to another without physical movement through space, in a manner similar to that depicted in the *Star Trek*, when Scotty beams up starship personnel with his matter transporter. If teleportation was the means by which three men and a broken-down transit van were conveyed across 170 miles of space, what type of power was responsible for the act? Jimmy Powell vaguely recalled a strange standing stone, or ley stone, near Wolverhampton. At the destination near Canterbury there was just such a stone standing nearby. Could the three men and their run-down vehicle have been teleported across England via the ley-line alignment that is known as the Canterbury Line? This line joins up ancient wells, Neolithic burial mounds, churches, standing stones and curiously, Wembley Stadium. Some believe that the name Wembley mean Womb of the leys – a place where ley-lines converge perhaps?

Canterbury, the cradle of Christianity in Saxon England, is positioned on a site that had already been revered by the ancients, 350 years before the arrival of the Romans in AD 43. Just what existed on the site of Canterbury cathedral in the era of the ancient megalith builders is still unknown, but the location was apparently regarded as sacred to the practitioners of a long-forgotten nature-based belief system, and it may have some geographical bearing on the vast network of alignments that criss cross the country. Several students of these alignments have postulated that the mysterious people who created them may have been tapping into some form of 'earth energy' and that the standing stones – found across the British Isles and continental Europe – may be analogous to the pylons of the National Grid. Could some unknown energy, that is perhaps amplified or focused by the standing stones, have teleported the transit van to the heart of rural Kent via the Canterbury Line? This scenario may have happened before with megalithic alignments.

A case from the 1970s was reported to me some years ago involving 32-year-old Jack Fraser and his 22-year-old fiancée Mona Lewis. Jack Fraser was the black sheep of his family. His two older brothers, Ron and Charles, were successful self-employed businessmen, and Jack's younger sister Hannah, had just left university and was about to move to London to set up her own jewellery-design business. In the autumn of 1975, Jack, who had been unemployed for two years, obtained a job stacking supermarket shelves, and felt great earning a wage for himself and Mona, who he planned to marry the following year. Jack visited his family home on Booker Avenue in Mossley Hill one November evening in 1975 to tell his father he was not only working, but was engaged to his beloved Mona, who hailed from Dovecot. The cold reception Jack received was unexpected. His father sneered at his lowly job, and Jack's mother seemed to look down on Mona and made condescending jokey remarks about Dovecot. By 10.15pm, Jack had had enough, and grabbing Mona by the hand, he dragged her from the sofa and out of the house, vowing never to return. Outside, a November fog was slowly covering Liverpool like ethereal lava, and into the blinding night vapours, Jack stormed off with Mona. He tried to get his bearings in the fog, whilst Mona cried at some of the hurtful things Jack's mother had said about her. Jack hugged her, telling her that she was the best thing that had ever happened to him.

The couple walked up Booker Avenue in their search for Mather Avenue, but it was nowhere to be found and the fog was starting to aggravate Mona's asthma. Suddenly, through the mists, Jack saw the quite unexpected but welcome sight of traffic lights at the junction of Picton, Wellington and Rathbone Roads – in Wavertree! Mona, not being familiar with the areas of Wavertree and Mossley Hill, did not appreciate the distance they had covered in the past few minutes – almost four miles, which was impossible. Jack checked his watch. He had left his parents' home on Booker Avenue at 10.15pm, and at 10.22pm he and Mona had somehow reached a street that was almost four miles from Booker Avenue. The mystery later deepened when Mike, a friend of Jack's, said he had been walking down the High Street in Wavertree on his way to the Wellington pub, when he had seen Jack and Mona literally appear in front of him outside the library.

Just before Jack and Mona found themselves in Wavertree, they would have passed a very curious ancient landmark, at the corner of Booker Avenue and Archerfield Road – the so-called Robin Hood's Stone – an upright slab of sandstone almost eight feet tall, which, until 1928, had stood 198 feet away in a field called Stone Hey. The Robin Hood's Stone (so called because legend has it that it was once used for archery practice) is thought to belong to the so-called Calder

Stones, a group of six ancient stones inscribed with mysterious marks and symbols that probably formed part of a Neolithic chief's 4000-year-old burial mound. The Calder Stones were first excavated around 1765 at a crossroads in Allerton, and some local historians have wrongly assumed that the district of Calderstones derived its name from these stones. In fact, Calderstone is an old Lancashire family name, and a Farmer Calderstone once owned land in Allerton. Today you will find the Calder Stones hidden away in rather lacklustre glass enclosures in Calderstones Park.

So, in 1975, we have an apparent teleportation in close proximity to a standing stone, but could there possibly be a similar stone in Wavertree? Well, in the grounds of Wavertree Library, close to the spot where Jack and Mona found themselves that foggy night, there lies a boulder far more ancient than the Calder Stones. The Wavertree Boulder, which is almost a ton in weight, was found in Gypsy Lane many years ago. Technically described by geologists as andesitic agglomerate, the boulder had been transported here from Cumbria by glaciers several millions of years ago.

Could some unknown energy linking the two ancient stones in Mossley Hill and Wavertree have been responsible for teleporting Jack Fraser and his fiancée across four miles of space?

THE HEADLESS HORSEMAN OF STADT MOERS PARK

As most people know, Stadt Moers Park in Whiston was developed from 1983 when Knowsley Council decided to turn a former 220-acre landfill site into a beautiful green oasis. The name Stadt Moers was chosen because Knowsley was twinned with the town of Moers in Germany. Now, when any ancient ground or certain old dwellings are disturbed, supernatural activity is often stirred up, and this was the case during the early development of Stadt Moers Park.

Around 1982, two 11-year-olds Ben and Sean were witnesses to a terrifying apparition near the old landfill site. A missing child is every parent's nightmare, and when Ben didn't return to his Huyton home on Manor Farm Road, his parents, John and Kathy, were frantic, and went to the police station after searching the neighbourhood until 11pm. They also rang Ken and Liz, Sean's parents over in Whiston, who were equally worried, because their lad hadn't been home yet either. Ken said the pair had gone out on their BMX bikes at 7.30pm and had not been seen since. John and Kathy teamed up with Sean's parents and went in search of their missing sons, and in Prescot's Warrington Road, a 13-year-old boy named Craig said he'd seen the boys on their bikes near St Nicholas's Church off Windy Arbor Road, at about 9pm. They all piled into Ken's Cortina, and within minutes were outside the church. As they got out of the car, they the clip-clop of a horse's hooves nearby. There was a full moon that night and a ground mist rolling eerily over the gravestones. Then a familiar young voice cried out, 'Mum!' Kathy spotted Ben peeping round a large black granite headstone. He came from behind the gravestone pushing his BMX. In an excited voice, he said: 'A man on a horse chased me and Sean by the 'oller (the slang-name for the landfill site) and I don't know where Sean's gone!'

'Where in God's name have you been?' asked Kathy, holding back tears as she flew towards her son.

'You've had your mother in tears, you, you gallivanting ...' John shouted at his son, but Ken and Liz were naturally more concerned about the whereabouts of their own son, and Ken asked Ben where he'd seen Sean last.

'By the black path,' was his reply, but no one knew what he was referring to, so he showed them. It turned out to be a narrow cinder-track leading to the landfill site, and sure enough, there was Sean – minus his beloved BMX bike. Liz ran to him and hugged him, and the boy babbled incoherently about 'a man with no head' who had chased him and Ben on horseback from the 'oller to the graveyard of St Nicholas's church. The boys' accounts of the headless rider, who had swung a sword at them during the pursuit, matched perfectly. Sean had been so terrified he had abandoned his bike to escape the homicidal horseman. When Ken went to retrieve the bike, he saw that the back tyre had been deeply slashed, as though by some long-bladed weapon, but the most terrifying thing was yet to come. After squashing into the Cortina, they drove up Windy Arbor Road, and when they came to the junction at Lickers Lane, they were confronted by a man on horseback coming from the opposite direction. Sean screamed, instantly recognising the equestrian figure. 'It's the man with no head!' shouted Ben. His father said 'Don't be daft, son, it's just someone out late riding their horse.'

The rider overtook the Cortina then swiftly turned and charged, holding a sword aloft! As the figure passed in front of the rising full moon, it was plain for all to see that he had no head. Liz and Kathy screamed as the horse thundered past and something struck the roof of the car. John and Ken tried to calm their wives, but when the weird figure turned and charged again, Ken swerved the Cortina violently down Lickers Lane and stepped on the accelerator to put as much distance between the vehicle and the supernatural entity. That headless horseman has been seen in the Whiston area since the 1890s, when Tushingham's Brickworks occupied the site of Stadt Moers Park, but who he was, and why he's headless is still unknown.

TIMESLIPS

In the summer of 1977, the Plessey Factory on Wilson Road in Huyton went on strike for over six weeks. Its 350 workers were striking over proposed redundancies, and I think the Plessey plant up in Kirkby was also on strike at this time over the same issues. Anyway, one of the striking workers at the Huyton factory, a man we shall call Steve, from Whiston, decided he'd had enough after four weeks of striking, and walked out of the Wilson Road plant. His 14-year-old son David saw him striding across farmland in the direction of Prescot. David was playing truant, or sagging as we used to say in those days, and he didn't want his father to find out, and yet he was curious as to where he was going. In the end, his father spotted him. David asked where he was going and Steve replied, 'I don't know,

I've had enough, lad,' and kept on walking. It was a beautiful hot June day, but Steve felt his future was being threatened by the strike, and he had also found himself drifting away from his wife over the past few months. He feared he was having a breakdown. On a sudden whim, he decided to take David to the old pub where he had first met the boy's mother – The Unicorn in Cronton village, which dates back to 1752.

After quite a few miles Steve and his son could no longer recognise the area around Cronton village, and found themselves in great expanses of unfamiliar fields. Without warning, the summer fields were turning white, and the temperature started to drop dramatically. Steve took his denim jacket off and put it round David, who was now shivering. 'Dad, why's it gone dead cold? Is that *snow*?' he asked, and Steve was lost for an answer. The further east they walked, the colder it became and soon they were trudging through snow-covered fields – in the middle of June! Father and son had grave misgivings about the dramatic change in the weather, but then things got even stranger.

Steve wondered whether it would be wiser to retrace their steps, but there was now thick fog in that direction, and he sensed he shouldn't enter it, so he decided to head south-west, towards Ditton, and hopefully within about half an hour they would reach a pub he knew, but when they got there, they were confronted by a very odd sight. In the middle of one of the snowy fields, were horses drawing nine old-fashioned ploughs, surrounded by crowds of cheering people, and when they got close enough, they saw that the people were all dressed like yokels in smocks and jerkins and strange hats and talked in a peculiar lingo. Steve felt as if he shouldn't approach them, but the cold was now bitter and he was worried about young David, so he threw caution to the wind and walked into the outdated crowd. An old man in a black quaker-type hat offered Steve a bottle of something. Steve smelt it and thought it was whisky. He took a swig and felt it burn his mouth. He told David to take a small sip, which set him coughing.

The man asked Steve where he had travelled from, and Steve

said, 'Huyton'. The man nodded, eyeing his clothes suspiciously, then started talking about the ploughing match, though most of his sentences were unintelligible. The nearest shelter was an inn, which Steve thought looked vaguely familiar. It was only when they were inside warming themselves by the fire that he realised that he and his son had somehow gone into the past. The people in the inn were in Victorian dress, and the innkeeper was like a character out of *Pickwick Papers*, but the log fire was a godsend. Everyone in the inn seemed fascinated by Steve and his son. David asked his dad where they were. 'I don't know, but we're leaving, come on,' said Steve.

'We're not going back out there are we? We'll catch our death.'

But Steve felt something bad would happen if he stayed, and grabbing David's arm, walked out of the inn and past the ploughing match. As they approached the swirling fog, he said the Lord's Prayer to himself. David almost collapsed with the cold, and his father scooped him up, and carried him over his shoulder. The fog thinned and cleared, and the next thing they could hear cars on the motorway. The skies were clear blue, and the heat of 1977 hit him.

I researched the case, and discovered that on the snowy Tuesday of 14 January 1862, on the land south of Cronton, on the outskirts of old Ditton, there was indeed a ploughing match – with nine competing ploughs, just as Steve describes – and nearby there was an old pub, the Ball Inn, possibly the Ball of Ditton. How on earth a depressed, striking worker from Plesseys in 1977 and his son could take a stroll to a place 115 years back in time is a complete mystery. Perhaps when Steve 'let go' of his life in 1977, on the verge of a breakdown, he had somehow let go of all the concerns that keep us anchored to the present, and in doing so, freed his mind to travel into the past.

And now for another intriguing timeslip.

The following true story was told to me a few years ago at the studios of Radio Merseyside by a listener named Doug, who died in January 2011. The phenomenon described within the story is well-known to me, and the greatest physicists in the world are only now cottoning on to it after ridiculing the idea behind it for so long.

It was a very unusual day to begin with. Billy Butler and the Tuxedos had top billing at the Cavern club, and the Undertakers were playing the lunchtime sessions, while over 20,000 people took to the streets that summer's day in July 1964. The Beatles were returning to their city in a homecoming of an almost religious kind; in fact, some were even saying the world-shaking Fab Four had been predicted in the Bible's Book of Revelation (9:8) as the Four Men with the hair of women, who created a sound that was louder than thundering horses. Beatles fanatics were even seeing prophetic references to Lennon in James Joyce's *Finnegan's Wake*. The Beatles were in town to be honoured in a civic reception at the Town Hall before attending the northern premiere of *A Hard Day's Night* at the Odeon on London Road, and with 20,000 fans of every age lining the streets to catch a glimpse of the most famous men in the world, it seemed the perfect time to 'go on the rob'.

Doug had hatched the idea of the robbery four days before, and now he and his dim-witted accomplice, Gerry, were about to embark on the job which would net them thousands. The target was a certain city-centre shop in a quiet corner of Park Lane, where eccentric 40-something Neil Tottie lived. He was a known tax-dodger and miser who hoarded cash in biscuit tins in his lodgings above his shop. His only frivolity was being a Beatles fan, and today he was one of the multitudes crowding the streets. In a pub five days previously, Doug had overheard Tottie telling a friend that he would be out to see the Beatles come Friday. Doug and Gerry climbed over the backyard of the shop and used nothing more sophisticated than a lolly-ice stick to jiggle open the old window catch.

Once inside Doug located the dark musky-smelling bedroom and groped under the bed, where 15 Huntley & Palmer biscuit tins were packed solid with banknotes. 'What d'you think you're doing?' screamed Neil Tottie, rising from his bed with vivid red spots all over his face – symptoms of chicken pox – and pulled an old Luger pistol from under his pillow and pointed it at Doug, who was still on his knees at the foot of the bed. Gerry put his hands in the air and his teeth chattered. 'Now, where've I seen you before?' Neil asked, his free hand scratching the scarlet spots on his nose. 'Ah, that's it; in the Vines, and your partner in crime here.'

Doug was lost for words, then said, 'Fair enough, Tottie, you caught us red-handed.'

'I'll say I bleedin' well did, and now you're going to pay,' was Tottie's chilling reply, 'I've always wanted to shoot someone, and now I've got the perfect excuse!'

'Don't be daft, Tottie, you'll hang.' Doug stared wide-eyed down the barrel of the Luger ... saw the trigger finger twitch ... then heard the bang.

Doug closed his eyes a second before the Luger, which was pointed at his chest, fired. He heard the bang and felt a blast of air against his face. Had his eyes remained open, he'd have seen the badly-maintained World War 2 pistol explode and Neil Tottie's index finger fly across the room. Gerry, standing beside him with his arms in the air, saw it all and thanked his lucky stars. Neil Tottie rolled on his bed screaming, blood spraying from his finger socket. Doug and Gerry ran out of the room and down the stairs to the front door, which was bolted. As Gerry stooped to unbolt it, Doug took a peek through the letterbox to check if the coast was clear. There stood a burly policeman peering up at the bedroom window, obviously having heard the pistol explode.

The housebreakers were forced to flee via the back door, and as they entered the backyard, the fine blue July skies darkened suddenly as if a solar eclipse was in progress. They stepped on to a barrel and climbed over the wall into a warren of foul-smelling alleyways. When they finally emerged they found themselves in an unfamiliar area of the city. The first thing they saw was an old-fashioned shop with a grimy sign advertising: O Williams Spirit Merchant. All of the roads were cobbled, the pavements narrow, and everywhere could be heard the clatter of horses' hooves and carriage wheels on the cobbles.

'Doug, where are we?' Gerry asked nervously. Gerry was a big burly man, but was deemed mentally deficient, or 'backward' as they said in those unenlightened days, but Doug had learned that his friend had some sort of psychic sense, well beyond normal human intuition, and always sensed danger before it arrived.

Two small men in black wide-brimmed hats, knee-length coats and pale straight trousers approached, talking in an unfamiliar accent, maybe a country Lancashire accent, and they looked Doug and Gerry up and down and smirked as they passed. Perhaps they found their drainpipe trousers and black leather jackets odd, for at this point, the two criminals did not even realise they had gone back in time to the Park Lane of 1860.

The luckless pair strolled along Park Lane, and for a moment, Doug thought they'd been whisked to old London when he saw a massive domed building in the distance which looked like St Paul's Cathedral. This was in fact the dome of the Customs House, a building that would be destroyed in the Blitz. The penny dropped when they noticed that the passers-by were dressed in Dickensian fashion. A boy stood on the corner of the street, selling newspapers. Doug approached him and asked to see one of the newspapers. The boy was taken aback by their appearance and with a look of pure astonishment, handed Doug a copy of the *Liverpool Mercury* dated 23 September 1860. Doug read the date with a palpitating heart and strange flickering sensation in his left cheek. He handed it back to the boy and turned round, determined to walk back the way they had come, but it was not to be.

Doug's instinct told him that he should retrace his steps to the alleyway on Park Lane, which, God willing, would return them to their own time, but suddenly a runaway wagon came hurtling down the street, pulled along by a horse with bulging eyes. The driver had fallen off on to the cobbled road and cracked open his skull. Now the wagon, which was stocked with sacks, was careering towards a little golden-haired child who was sitting on the edge of the kerb, oblivious to her impending death.

Doug belted down the uneven pavement towards the child, scooped her up in his arms, and leapt out of the way in the nick of time. Gerry threw himself into a doorway as the horse's body twisted and fell as the wagon tipped over and smashed into the bow window of the shop. A crowd gathered around the whinneying horse, which had somehow fallen into the cellar of an ale house through two wooden trap doors and was now trapped. A smaller knot of people stood helplessly around the driver of the wagon as he bled to death on the cobbles further up Park Lane.

The child sobbed in Doug's arms, and he rocked her and said, 'There there, love, you're okay now.' Gerry approached him and a woman, who was only about five feet in height also came running towards Doug, and in an Irish accent cried, 'Maggie, my dear,' and to Doug, 'Oh thank you, thank you sir,' as she scooped the child from his arms. Doug and Gerry hurried on down the alleyway at the back of Park Lane, and prepared to climb the yard wall which, hopefully, had 1964 on the other side. Gerry suddenly said to his friend, 'Hey, look who that is!' And he pointed to a man in a hat like the one of the old rosy-cheeked man found on a box of Quaker Oats porridge. He sucked on a clay pipe and grinned at the two men. It was an old tramp Doug and Gerry knew only by the nickname of Charlie Chuck. Back in their time, the tramp was always scruffily dressed, but now here he was wearing fine clothes and sporting the gold chain of a fob watch in his silk waistcoat.

'Come on, Gerry,' urged Doug. They climbed the wall, jumped down into the yard, and immediately the sky changed from being overcast to a bright cloudless blue. They were home, but more problematically they were back in the yard of Tottie's shop. They quickly climbed over an adjacent wall and were soon walking the streets of Liverpool, through the crowds of the 20,000 people that had turned out for the Beatles homecoming. Doug was intrigued by the presence of that tramp from his era being in the Liverpool of 1860. Gerry said he might have just looked like Charlie Chuck or was perhaps his great-grandfather, but Doug thought it was odd how no one ever saw that tramp again, nor knew what had become of him. Had he perhaps stumbled through that time-barrier at the back of Park Lane and found a better life a century ago, armed with the knowledge of today perhaps?

Doug told me this story in 2008, and died not long afterwards.

His daughter says she's convinced it happened because Doug had told her the story so many times over the years. If you know where to look, you too may find a door to the past.

The following timeslip is unusual as it seemed to provide a glimpse of the future.

In the 1950s Watt's bakery stood on Heyworth Street in Everton. I don't know exactly where it stood, but one cold morning in 1956, 32-year-old Billy Stanley from West Derby had a row with his wife over his constant gambling on the horses, and stormed out of the house, on his way to his mother's off Breck Road. Billy's mother happened to be at the launderette when he called, so Billy went to Watt's bakery and bought himself a hot Scouse pie for breakfast, and he walked along Everton Road, scoffing it. This man, Billy Stanley, was a very simple soul. He had no interest in ghosts, the supernatural, or anything outside of his everyday world of Bernard Murphy betting shops, the alehouse, the pawnbroker, and the opposite sex.

On this particular morning, when he looked up from his Scouse pie, he got the shock of his life, because he found himself in a place that was initially unfamiliar. Then he realised that somehow, Liverpool had been decimated, either by war or some natural catastrophe. Entire streets were missing – whole districts had vanished, replaced by fields strewn with rubble. The church of St Chrysostom stood in the middle of all of this desolation, as if it had been spared by whoever it was that had bombed Everton. It reminded Billy of the devastation he'd witnessed in the May Blitz of 1941. Then he saw his auntie's house, and his heart skipped a beat, because it was empty, and its roof missing. Dirty ragged curtains flapped about as Billy looked through the smashed windows. He started to panic, thinking something terrible had happened to the city – perhaps an H Bomb had been dropped, but he couldn't understand how he'd never heard any explosion.

Then Billy saw an odd-looking police car driving down a road that went straight through this desert of dereliction. The vehicle was much smaller than a normal car, and had strange black and white

76

panels on it. At this point, elderly Jimmy Mercer came upon the scene, and let out a string of expletives coughing violently. 'What the heck, Billy? Oh my God? What's happened?'

Billy shook his head, and the old man said, 'Look, there's only the church still standing and the old Everton water tower.'

At this point, another person, named Tony Upton turned up. He was a former neighbour of Billy's, and he was visibly shaken at the moonscape that stretched before him. He had first noticed something wasn't right as he walked up Breck Road. A kind of fog had covered everything west of Everton Road for about a mile, but this fog cleared within a minute to reveal that half of Everton was missing. Tony said he had also seen a boy of about ten, in weird bell-bottom trousers, and this boy had strange long hair and a black and white chequer-board patterned jersey. He had seemed terrified, and ran off. All three men, walked in stunned silence up Everton Road, and as soon as they came to Northumberland Terrace, all the missing streets slowly returned.

Billy Stanley often told this story before he passed away in the 1980s, and the two other men also told their family and friends about the incident, which has to be a timeslip into the future, because, as most people from the Everton area will know, half of Everton was bulldozed in the sixties and seventies and those who remember the so-called slum-clearances will tell you that the vast stretches of bulldozed streets around the Everton Road area were just fields of rubble, and St Chrysostom's church was indeed left standing in the middle of nowhere with only the Everton water tower for company. The boy in the chequer-board jersey was most likely a typical child of the 1970s. Billy Stanley said this incident took place around 1957-58, because he recalled that the father of actor Ricky Tomlinson worked in Watt's bakery on Heyworth Street around this time. I wonder if any readers out there can confirm this?

In early June 2011, 17-year-old Imogen from Garston went to Liverpool City Centre to buy a few things for her older sister Abigail, who had just become a mum. Imogen was pleasantly surprised to see that a new branch of Mothercare had opened on the corner of Lord Street and Whitechapel, and eagerly ventured into the store and bought some baby things for her sister, all of which were incredibly low-priced. Imogen imagined they were being sold at introductory bargain prices because the store had just opened – until she tried to pay with her credit card. The girl behind the counter eyed the card with suspicion, then went to a senior member of staff and showed it her. She put on her glasses and peered closely at the card, shook her head, and handed it back to Imogen. 'We don't take those, love,' she said. Imogen only had a small amount of cash on her, and so she put the items back, left the store, and went to Liverpool One. When she returned to Garston at teatime, she told her mum about the incident at Mothercare – and Debbie said there was no Mothercare on the corner of Lord Street. 'There used to be, but it moved years ago.'

'Well, it's back again,' said Imogen.

'Imogen, I should know, girl, 'cos I opened my new account at the HSBC Bank ... and it's where the old Mothercare used to be.'

Only when Imogen and her mother went to town the next day and she saw the bank with her own eyes did she accept that she had experienced something which I have studied and catalogued for many years – a timeslip. That explained why the credit card had been rejected and why the prices were so low – they seemed to have dated back to the early 1980s.

Bold Street seems to have the highest incidence of time-slippage in the city, and I have been mapping the areas of that street with magnetometers and various other electronic sensors with a view to perhaps inducing one of these timeslips. If I vanish into thin air one day you'll know I've succeeded.

Timeslips into the future are not as common as the ones into the past, but one of the most intriguing allegedly took place one Wednesday night in the Queensway Tunnel around 1957, when 44-year-old businessman Geoff Kingsley was driving to Birkenhead around 11.45pm. The tunnel was almost deserted and Mr Kingsley was alarmed when he saw something approaching from behind at high speed in the wing mirror of his Morris Minor. It looked like some sleek ultra-modern vehicle – triangular with rounded edges – and was golden. This futuristic vehicle bulleted past Kingsley's car at such a phenomenal speed, that the Morris Minor shuddered and was pulled sideways. The suicidal driver curved the mercurial vehicle into the tunnel wall, leaving skid-marks in his wake. This car was either ghostly, or the section of the tunnel wall into which it seemed to vanish was some sort of high-speed door – but a door to where? Mr Kingsley is but one of about a dozen people who have seen that golden car, which will probably come into production in our lifetime.

JOHN REID OF ANFIELD

In 1866 John Reid, a mere cabin boy and gopher with dreams of becoming a junior midshipman, and ultimately a captain, enlisted on a steam corvette of 21 guns, bound for the West Indies. A week out, butter-fingered Reid dropped a long-cherished bottle of the captain's Spanish rum, and it smashed to smithereens. Lashed to the turret of a gun, the officers whipped him until he passed out, and then someone – it was never determined just who – took a knife-blade to the boy's left cheek and engraved the shape of a heart. 'My heart bleeds for you, Reid!' mocked the knife-wielding officer. Gunpowder was poured over the etched wound and lit. The officers laughed at the screaming boy through the cloud of billowing smoke. He was now marked for life with the gunpowder tattoo.

Reid, of Scottish and Irish descent, hailed from Anfield, and after he had recovered from the whipping and facial disfigurement, he became a silent and angry young man who seemed bent on revenge against everyone. In the West Indies he studied Voodoo and African magic, and fell under the spell of old Nebus, a bokor, or Voodoo sorcerer, who tattooed Reid with all sorts of occult symbols. The heart etched on Reid's left cheek was coloured crimson by Nebus's needles, and then the African shaman tattooed diamonds, clubs and spades on the young man's shaven head. Nebus said that if Reid ever wanted money, he had only to rub the diamond symbol on his temple, and if he wanted love, he should rub his finger gently on the heart on his face and think of the object of his affection. To curse someone with death and illness, Reid would only have to look at or visualise the victim, and touch the spade symbol on his forehead three times. Death would surely follow. Reid hungered for more powers, and so the bokor tattooed the much-feared Evil Eye symbol around his left eye. Now if Reid shut his right eye and stared through the Evil Eye, he could bring long-lasting bad luck and tragedy to anyone or anything. Some of the other symbols and tattoos included that of a baby, which women only had to touch to become pregnant, and a black pentagram which Reid could use to invoke a personal powerful demon in times of danger. Reid even had an eye in a triangle tattooed on to the back of his head so he would be aware of things going on behind his back.

John Reid returned to Liverpool and finally tracked down the five officers from the corvette who had mocked him when he was whipped, and he glared at them collectively with the Evil Eye. Within days, the ship they boarded for Philadelphia was lost at sea. Eventually, the bokor's voodoo magic wore off, and John Reid in his older, mellower days, would sit in pubs like the King Harry in Anfield, and satisfy the curious with his tales of adventure around the globe. A woman who was said to have been infertile, rubbed the baby tattoo on Reid's arm and later had twins. Years after John Reid died, his ghost was often seen in the King Harry, and some think his spirit still haunts his favourite watering hole.

THE NYMPH OF THE DINGLE

Facing Waterstones bookstore, the grand Lyceum stands disgracefully derelict at the bottom of Bold Street, but over a hundred years ago, on a stormy January afternoon, a rather heated discussion was taking place within the walls of that magnificent building, which was then a library and a gentleman's club frequented by moneyed merchants. The discussion in the Lyceum's newspaper reading room concerned the 'eternal subject' – that of ghosts. A broker named Bennett clumsily paraphrased a quatrain by the Persian poet Omar

Khayyam: 'Strange is it not? That of the myriad people who pass through the Door of Darkness, not one returns to tell us of that road that we must travel ourselves one day.'

'Perhaps some who die have returned, and they are the ghosts we hear of,' mused Carden, a captain in the Coldstream Guards. He lowered his gaze as he sucked on his cigar and pretended to study *The Times* newspaper, knowing full well his controversial comments would stoke the debate.

'Only one returned from the tomb.' said a religious Welsh shipwright by the name of Williams.

'Lazarus did too, and that woman Tabitha,' quipped Samuel Hollinson, a professor of music, 'if the Bible is to be believed.'

Williams was stuck for words, but then a financier named Carson interposed: 'Jones has met a ghost, haven't you, Jonesy?' and he looked over at an irritated Glynn Jones, a cotton broker. 'Oh shut it,' Jones said, and hid his face behind the broadsheet he was reading. But the other club members finally coaxed him into talking about his supernatural experience. Here is the outline of his strange tale.

One summer in the 1880s, Jones became ill from overwork at the Cotton Exchange, and his physician prescribed a full week of rest in a rural setting. Jones went to stay with his widowed Aunt Margaret, who lived in a cottage overlooking a picturesque glen in the valley of the Dingle. Virtually cut off from civilisation, Jones began a gradual recuperation, and morning and evening he would ramble around the green wilds of the Dingle, following the now-vanished stream that meandered through a valley spangled with a spectrum of flowers, past ancient oaks and elms. Jones would reach Jericho Shore, before returning homeward amid the song of the greenfinch.

One evening, as a full moon turned the glens of the Dingle silver, Jones heard a beautiful female voice singing in a language he recognised as Gaelic – the tongue of his grandmother. Glynn Jones followed the song on the night-time air and it brought him to a strange but beautiful scene. A half-naked young woman stood demurely in the stream, singing of Mother Nature. Her hair was long and reddish-brown, crowned with yellow flowers above the fairest face Glynn had ever seen. Her breasts were bare, her skin the colour of moonlight, and a diaphanous veil hung from her waist to her knees. When Glynn approached she did not cover herself, but looked up and smiled at the young businessman. 'What is your name?' Glynn asked, blushing. She told him in Gaelic that her name was Eleetra. 'Where do you live, Eleetra?' Glynn enquired, but the vision of youth and beauty said she did not live. She was not alive at all.

Eleetra stood in the moonlit stream with her beautiful captivating eyes fixed on those of the lovelorn Glynn Jones. 'But surely you are alive, you are so lovely,' Glynn told the nymph.

Eleetra's eyebrows slanted with annoyance and her eyes flared with unearthly light, and in her ancient Gaelic tongue she said: 'Leíg leis na marbh laidhe!' – Let the dead lie!

'I'm sorry,' Glynn murmured, 'but I don't understand.'

Eleetra told him she was the manifestation of nature in the form of woman, and that she had never lived as a real mammalian person; she had never emerged from a womb to greet the world with a primal cry to the midwife, and she pointed to her pale smooth abdomen as she explained this. She had no navel; no umbilical cord had ever connected her to a mortal mother of flesh and blood. She told Glynn to take off his shoes and socks, to which he willingly complied. And then she held out her hand and he took it. Walking barefoot in the Dingle stream on this warm summer night with the most beautiful maiden on earth was a delight he could never have imagined.

Beneath the prehistoric moon and the eternal sentinel stars, the once-mundane cotton broker and a girl who had never been born ran splashing up the Dingle stream, watched by badger, fox, owl – and the eyes of the Unseen Folk that we humans know dimly as faeries. Glynn and Eleetra skipped through feathery broad-buckler ferns, through honey-scented pink and purple thyme, through meadows and valley, until they came to the rocky outcrop of Knott's Hole, which today lies beneath the site of the old Garden Festival. Here, Glynn declared his undying love for Eleetra, and kissed her for the first time. They looked out from the cave down to the Jericho Shore, where the ancient stream the Jordan flows into the river the Romans called Belisama. The Anglo-Saxons labelled it Maerse, and we know it as the Mersey. It will have other names when our race is done.

The lovers sat embracing in their cave beside the river, and Eleetra told the spellbound Glynn some of the secrets of nature, and how the whole earth is a living mother who feeds off the sun. Eleetra revealed that she had had two mortal lovers before Glynn. These were the renowned local historian, philanthropist and poet William Roscoe (who had passed away in 1831), and a young captain who was tragically lost at sea. Eleetra took Glynn to an alcove on Knott's Hole where Roscoe had installed a statue of his love, whom he called the Nymph of the Dingle. The significance of that statue mystified local historians for many years. It was vandalised and removed to the grounds of the nearby Turner Memorial Home and subsequently lost. Eleetra predicted the destruction of the beautiful Dingle countryside, and this all came to pass. In 1919 the whole of the Dingle estate was bought outright by the Mersey Docks and Harbour Board. An oil-refinery was built on the land, and jetties for the shipping of petroleum blotted the area. Trees were uprooted, and a wall was built across the Jericho Shore. The Dingle stream was culverted, and by the early 1960s the shore had vanished. Glynn Jones was forbidden by his priest to continue his affair with the supernatural 'Nymph of the Dingle', and the cotton broker had to be bound to his bed and sedated by a doctor until his 'mania' subsided.

THE SUPERNATURAL TROUBLESHOOTER

It was 4.20pm in May 1978 when 13-year-old Gemma settled down in front of the television to watch a show called *Paul*, presented by singer and actor Paul Nicholas. Gemma had a crush on Paul and was infuriated when the programme went off air after ten minutes. As the television blared out static, the ceiling shook, and the girl's 10-year-old brother Tony ran in to ask if she'd just heard the bang. At this time, Gemma and Tony's parents were still both at work, and when their mother arrived a minute later, Paul had returned to the television screen, and infatuated Gemma had forgotten all about the ceiling-jarring jolt. Gemma and her family lived in the top flat of a towerblock, and that night Tony went into his sister's room to complain that he could hear people walking about on the flat roof. 'Oh, don't be daft, Tony, what would anyone be doing on the roof at this time of night?' said Gemma, dismissively and Tony went out in a sulk.

The next day at midday Gemma decided to come home for her lunch, and just after noon, there was a knock at the door. She thought it might be her brother, but instead, a tall man with a grey basin-cut hairstyle stood there with a case in his hand. 'Is your mum or dad home?' he asked, with a slight Scottish lilt.

'No, why? Are you the clubman?' Gemma asked, thinking he might be Mr Newrick, the credit draper's, replacement.

'No, I'm no clubman, lassie. When will your parents be home? I'll call back.'

'My mum might be home soon, come in if you want,' said Gemma and the man smiled and stepped inside. Gemma asked if he wanted a cup of tea, but he shook his head and instead took a pair of headphones from his case and plugged them into a device that resembled a metal detector which he swept across the ceiling.

'What're you doing?' Gemma asked, concerned at the man's strange behaviour.

'Have you ever heard of UFOs?' the man asked. Gemma looked at him blankly. 'You know, lassie,' said the stranger, 'flying saucers and that?'

'Yeah, why?' Gemma was now regretting having let the man in.

The man took off his headphones and introduced himself with a smile. 'I'm Clive by the way.'

'I'm Gemma. What's your job?'

'That's a good question, Gemma,' said Clive and took a minute before answering: 'I'm a supernatural troubleshooter I suppose. You have a bona fide flying saucer on your roof.'

Clive said he lived in a flat on the top floor of Entwistle Heights, a mile away, and with his special high-magnification binoculars, he had seen the craft land on top of the flats the day before. Clive said these particular UFOs were hostile, and that this one was being hunted by military forces from another planet. At this point, Gemma's mother arrived home, and soon threw Clive out of the flat after calling him a crank. That night dozens of people saw a disc-shaped craft, 30 feet in diameter, rise from that block of flats and accelerate skywards until it shrank to a star-like point then vanished.

I have heard of Clive before. He is said to be a far-sighted scientist who helped develop RADAR systems during the Second World War, as well as working on a device to incapacitate German aircraft by sending high-powered beams of short-wave energy to interfere with the engine's workings. Clive also seriously hypothesised a terrifying weapon that could destroy the Solar System back in 1955, and even drew up the plans, which were thankfully scrapped. Clive's blueprints were of a huge bank of gamma-ray lasers which could induce the sun to explode, or go supernova. Clive suggested developing the weapon to destroy the home suns of any invading hostile aliens in times to come, and suggested trying the Death Star-type weapon out on Epsilon Eridani, a star that lies ten and a half light years away from us. Thankfully, as far as I know, the starbuster lasers were never built!

Parasitic Things

This is one of the most bizarre stories I've ever researched, and it may seem a bit far-fetched, but everything in it is rooted in fact and factual accounts that I've collected from people over a ten-year period. I'll start in chronological order.

In January 1972, over 280,000 mine-workers in Britain went on a seven-week strike after three months' of negotiation with the National Coal Board over a pay rise ended in deadlock. The Conservative government of the day was capping all pay rises to fight inflation, and so the miners resorted to industrial action and 289 pits across the land were closed. At that time, three quarters of the country's electricity was derived from coal-burning power stations, and the coal resources soon dwindled, necessitating power cuts to conserve fuel. Prime Minister Ted Heath declared a state of emergency. Cities were blacked out and over a million people were laid off work. The government enforced emergency restrictions to safeguard electricity supplies for essential services, and anyone found to be recklessly leaving lights on or needlessly using electricity was liable to a £100 fine or a three month prison term. Candles and storm lamps were even used in the House of Commons.

Now, on the night of one of these powercuts in January 1972, a couple left a pub in Edge Hill, and walked home down Spekeland Road, a very long and lonely road. Halfway down, a car passed them with its headlights blazing. This car had only travelled about 300 yards when it suddenly screeched to a halt. Its red brake lights came on and it started to reverse at high speed, stopping by the couple. The driver shouted out the window: 'Seen them down there?' The couple looked down the dark road in the direction of the driver's nod, and in the distance, were some weird-looking things darting about in the headlight's beams. They looked like huge spiders – and were coming towards the couple, who turned on their heels and ran off.

On the following evening, at dusk, one of these creatures was allegedly seen crossing Tunnel Road. It was said to have a brown egg-shaped body and three very spindly legs, about 2-3 feet in length, described as 'wiry and tentacle-like'. A policeman who retired in 1992 told me that in 1972, he was driving down Tunnel Road and saw one of these creatures; 'I saw something so fantastic I could hardly believe my eyes,' he recalled. 'This thing was walking with a peculiar gait across Tunnel Road, and I can only describe it as looking like a brown egg, about the size of a medium Easter egg, with three legs attached, as thin as macaroni. I tried to swerve around it but it seemed to fling itself into the path of the car. Out of curiosity I stopped and got out the car, expecting to see the thing flattened in the road, but there was nothing there. I drove on to Admiral Street police station, and halfway through the journey, I noticed the thing was stuck to my rear window with its legs pressed against the glass like a letter Y. I was that preoccupied with the thing, I went through a red light and almost hit another vehicle. When I reached Admiral Street station the thing was nowhere to be seen.'

Now for another account that dovetails with the two previous stories. In September 1974, 17-year-old Denise went out drinking with her friends, and then, in a drunken state, went with her boyfriend – and a couple of bottles of cider – to Newsham Park, where they kissed and cuddled. 'It was all very innocent,' says Denise, 'but then he started begging me to sleep with him and I said it was too soon.' They argued and the boyfriend stormed off, leaving Denise in a semi-comatose state. In the dark, Denise remembered falling on her back, and then, as she tried to get up, she felt something crawl on to her and slide into her mouth, and down her throat into her stomach. She panicked and got to her feet, choking, and retching. She thought a rat had got into her mouth, and somehow made it to the Royal Hospital on Pembroke Place, and all the way she could feel something writhing about in her stomach. At the Royal, a doctor told her to go home. He said no rat could have possibly crawled into her mouth, and that she'd hallucinated the whole thing through drink.

About a week later, Denise went to bed, and was sleeping soundly, when she was awakened by a strange snapping sound, and her mother's scream. Her mother had peeped into her bedroom to check on her and saw something resembling a worm hanging from Denise's mouth. This 'worm' was about two feet long and its end was touching the alarm clock. As soon as she screamed, the thing had snapped back into her mouth.

Denise was naturally terrified, and once again went to the Royal. This time a doctor said that perhaps a tape worm was living in her gut, and they x-rayed her, but the x-ray showed something very odd. A gastric expert said he had never seen anything like it before. It looked like three tape worms joined up in Denise's large colon. At this time Denise had symptoms identical to severe irritable bowel syndrome. A gastric specialist advised her to stay in the hospital for treatment, and she did, but on the second night, at around four in the morning, Denise had the horrible sensation that the thing inside her was about to leave via her anus.

The next morning the bedsheets were found to be soaked with blood and faecal matter. X-rays established that the thing had gone. A nurse at the hospital who happened to know a relative of Denise's later said she had seen something on the ward that night that gave her nightmares for years, but she was scared to say what she'd seen at the time because she would have probably lost her job. She claimed it had slithered out of the ward leaving behind a trail of blood. The nurse followed the trail and came upon a weird oval-shaped 'thing' with writhing tentacles, that was moving across the ground floor corridor leading to the hospital entrance. She went to fetch a matron, but when they returned, the thing had gone. These apparently parasitic creatures have been reported in other parts of the world since the 1950s, and even today they are still occasionally reported. Are they some mutation of an invertebrate animal or are they alien in origin?

THE SERPENT TATTOO

This strange story unfolded in October 1965. Around teatime, 23-year-old John Beckett sat in his flat on Gambier terrace, off Hope Street, watching *Scene at 6.30* on his black and white television set. His thoughts kept turning to a beautiful red-haired girl who worked in the Rushworth & Dreaper store on Whitechapel. John didn't even know the girl's name, but he was besotted with her, and planned to go into the shop any day soon to ask her out. There was only one problem, he was already engaged to marry Tina. On this particular night, John felt like staying in, and at half-past seven he was watching the comedy show *Here's Harry*, featuring the popular comedian Harry Worth. Anyway, John's friend, a beatnik type named Ian, who was into jazz and purple hearts, called at the flat and persuaded John to go out. The two men went to a local backstreet pub called Ye Cracke, on Rice Street (just off Hope Street), then on to another pub, ending up in the Lorne on Brownlow Hill. From there they went to the famous Mardi Gras club on Mount Pleasant, and who should John Beckett see at this nightclub but the object of his desire – the girl from Rushworth & Dreaper, merrily dancing away. John smiled at the girl, but she pretended not to notice, and at the end of the night he and Ian left the Mardi on their own. John was so drunk he was almost speechless, and to make matters worse, Ian suddenly copped off with a beautiful girl from Paddington and left him on Mount Pleasant.

John staggered up Mount Pleasant, passing the opticians A E Walsby, and here he saw an old fashioned shop window with glass bull's eye panes, and a red light burning inside. He looked through the window and saw an old bald-headed man, the spitting image of Alastair Sim, talking to a tall elegant woman who could have been a model. Her hair was piled up in a bun, Audrey Hepburn style, and she held a long cigarette holder as she chatted to the old man.

'What is this place?' John Beckett muttered, and decided to go in. A sweet musky smell greeted his nose, and he saw the man examining a red-raw tattoo on the graceful woman's forearm. A heart with some symbol in it. 'Is this a tattoo parlour?' he asked. The old man nodded and smiled, and the tall slim woman slipped into the back of the shop, saying, 'You look as if you could do with some black coffee.'

'Oh I could,' said John, and the old man told him to take a seat and relax. John rambled on about the red-haired girl he had a thing for, and the old man smiled and said, 'Faint heart never won a fair lady. I have just the thing for you.' And he produced a huge leather-bound book full of tattoo illustrations and flipped to a page showing a long black snake. 'An ancient fertility tattoo worn by the Druids, the phallic serpent. The Druid priests made barren women pregnant when this symbol was inscribed into their flesh.'

'I don't know about that, mate, I'm a bit squeamish,' said John Beckett, nervously, but the female assistant reappeared with a cup of hot aromatic coffee, and proceeded to stroke his head. There was obviously something in that coffee, because John passed out minutes later, and when he came round he felt as if he was strapped down on some sort of bench, minus his shirt and vest, with an intense pain around his stomach. When he tried to scream, the woman smiled without moving her eyes and stuffed a wad of some sort in his mouth. The next thing John recalled was waking up in the doorway of the Hatbox Shop, just a few doors up from the Mardi Gras. It was almost light by now, and the buses were running.

John somehow staggered home to his flat on Gambier Terrace, and got the shock of his life when he looked in his wardrobe mirror. He had been tattooed with the image of a long black snake. The head of the snake was a few inches below his left nipple, and it ran in a curve, down past his belly button, so the tail went right down through his pubic hair to his penis. He was in agony, and decided to report what had happened to the police, but all he got from the desk sergeant was, 'You're not a kid are you? You knew what you were doing didn't you? You must have paid him. Why did you go into the parlour in the first place if you didn't want to be tattooed?'

John tried to find the tattoo parlour on Mount Pleasant in broad daylight, without success. It should have been between Walsby's the opticians and the Hat Box, but there was no shop with bull's eyes windows to be seen, so no one believed John's story. However, a night watchman guarding roadworks on Upper Newington later told John that he had seen him enter the shop in question.

Anyway, from that day onwards a change in John Beckett's nature began to take place and he became a determined womaniser. His first move was to boldly walk into Rushworth & Dreaper and asked the red-headed girl out. Her name was Jeanette and she turned him down but he refused to take no for an answer, and in the end she caved in and went out with him. Within months she was pregnant and the same week, John's long suffering girlfriend, Tina, also became pregnant. During this time, John had been seeing no less than four other women.

In the summer of 1966, Tina was taken to Oxford Street Maternity Hospital, and who should be in next bed to her, but Jeanette. Both girls ended up in tears with John sitting between their beds, his face in his hands. The nurses were disgusted by him, especially when he even tried it on with one of them. Tina gave birth to a baby girl, and later noticed a birthmark on the infant's back like a little snake, and Jeanette's baby is also said to have been born with an identical birthmark. John Beckett turned to the church, because he feared he was on the road to becoming a rapist, such was the inferno of lust that had him in its grasp. After moving into a certain priest's house, John slowly reverted to becoming a decent person again, and the tattoo eventually faded away over time, something a normal tattoo can never do, because a tattoo is literally a coloured scar.

John recalled how during his lecherous period he had developed a hunger for the hottest curries he could find, and even more bizarrely, a ravenous urge for raw or undercooked meat. Whilst waiting for his breakfast at a cafe on Church Street one morning, he barged into the kitchen and aggressively demanded that the young cook serve him some blood-red bacon. He also found himself continually thirsting for the most mature and strongest whisky and started to chew tobacco – even though he only rarely smoked before the tattoo incident. The serpent tattoo is one of those cases in my files which really stumps me, for I can offer no rational explanation.

THREE WOMEN

In the early summer of 1960, freelance news photographer Jason St Michael happened to be at the scene of a fatal car crash near London Road. Being a professional, Jason carried his camera at all times, as opportunity seldom knocks twice. On this day he took several photographs of the crash and sold prints to several newspapers, including the *Daily Post* and *Liverpool Echo*. When he was in the darkroom of his apartment on Falkner Street, he noticed something intriguing. Among the crowd of people gawping at the crashed car with its dead driver, were three women, all aged about 40-something, and each wearing a black headscarf tied in a knot under the chin. All three looked foreign, sallow-skinned, with prominent aquiline noses. Jason estimated their heights to be roughly the same – about six feet tall, which was truly exceptional for a woman in those days. Jason then scrutinised another photograph he had taken of an accident at New Brighton fairground the year before, when a girl of twelve fell off a Ferris wheel and was almost killed. In that photograph, amongst the crowd of morbid onlookers and sensation-seekers, were the same three women in black headscarves.

Intrigued by this coincidence, Jason obtained permission to browse through the photographic archives of the local newspapers, and straight away, spotted the three mysterious women in a picture of an horrendous accident near the docks, too graphic to be printed in the newspapers, of man crushed to death by stone blocks that had fallen from a wagon. Amongst the gaggle of bystanders staring at the ghastly scene, was a woman with her young son. She had turned her son's face away, but standing next to them, clear as day, were those three women in the black headscarves and knee-length light coloured mackintoshes. They seemed to be grinning, and in this clearer picture, Jason noticed their strong facial similarities, and it looked as if they were sisters.

Jason told a news editor about the three women, but he could see nothing particularly mysterious about them. People always gathered round the scene of accidents, and lots of women wore headscarves – so what? They weren't the same three women in every photograph – how could they be? Jason sensed that the editor was actually superstitious, and was in fact rather frightened by the women.

About a fortnight later, Jason St Michael was taking pictures of tramps at the back of St Luke's Church one sunny afternoon, hoping to sell them to a London pictorial magazine that was doing a series on Liverpool street life, when suddenly he overheard some women passing by talking about a 'big fire on Church Street'. Quickly dropping what he was doing, he headed for Church Street. As he was hurrying down Bold Street, he saw a towering column of black smoke reaching skywards. This was obviously a major blaze. On reaching Hanover Street, he could see flames and smoke billowing from the upper floors of Hendersons, and the fire engines in the street amidst a tangle of red hosepipes. The police hadn't yet cordoned off the street, but as Jason started taking photographs, they arrived, and started pushing the crowds back away from the blaze. Jason caught everything, including the dreadful spectacle of a man falling to his death from a ledge where he had just led some women from the blazing upper storeys of Hendersons to the safety of a neighbouring roof.

In the middle of all this drama, Jason spotted them – the same three women in the black headscarves – their eyes glued to the poor souls on the ledge of the burning building. Jason had to get to them to find out just who these three ghouls were. He squeezed through the crowd and was eventually standing right behind them. As he considered the best angle from which to photograph them, all three suddenly turned round to face him. In close up, their faces were weird; like men in heavy make up, their jet black eyes bulging, and pure hatred was etched on each face. Jason got the distinct impression that the trio knew he had cottoned on to them. He felt he was looking at angels of death, and backed away into the crowd, fearing for his life. Everyone else was engrossed in the unfolding tragedy of the Hendersons fire, so were unaware of the three women in their midst. Jason headed off towards Paradise Street, and didn't feel safe until he was in the doorway of Coopers.

Three months later, Jason went into Lewis's and entered the elevator with a large group of shoppers, but the attendant said there were too many passengers and asked for three people to leave. Jason then received a horrible jolt, for there, in the corner, stood those same three creepy women. He hurried out of the lift and the attendant asked two of these women if they too would mind stepping out, as most of the other passengers were elderly. Two of the women reluctantly left the elevator, then the third followed, even though the attendant said she didn't have to. Jason was convinced that he had prevented the terrifying threesome from causing another disaster at Lewis's, and he quickly left the store as they fixed him with expressions of pure hatred. They followed him along Ranelagh Street, as far as the top of Bold Street, where he lost them in the crowds, but this was not to be the last time that Jason would have an encounter with those sinister women.

In 1962, he was driving along Western Avenue in Speke when he was involved in a head-on collision with a Ford Zodiac. The steering wheel was almost embedded in his chest after the impact, and he crawled from the smashed car as a crowd gathered around. The last thing he saw before passing out was the three women with the black head-scarves staring down at him amongst the crowd of onlookers. When Jason woke up in hospital, a surgeon told him he'd probably imagined the women because he was suffering from severe shock, and thankfully, Jason never saw them again. Who they were, and why they always seemed to be the first on the scene of any tragedy remains a mystery.

After I had discussed this case on the radio one afternoon, the receptionist at the station came into the studio after the broadcast and told me there was a woman on the phone who wanted to talk to me about the three women. I took the call which was to an elderly woman named Margaret, who now lives in Knotty Ash. Margaret said that many years ago, in the 1970s, she had been walking down a certain street in Liverpool, when she saw something fall in front of her and hit the ground with an explosive sound. It was a human body, and blood and body tissue sprayed her and several vehicles parked nearby. A man had jumped off the nearby block of flats, and had hit the ground with such an impact, he was – to use Margaret's ghastly description – like 'a huge puddle of ketchup with clothes on top'. Reeling from witnessing what turned out to be a suicide, she staggered towards a parked car and leaned against it. She heard voices to her right, and turned to see three women standing close by, staring at the splattered corpse on the pavement. Each of their heads was covered by a headscarf, of the type for which Sophia Loren was famed, and they wore funereal clothes. But what struck Margaret as noticeably odd, even though she was quite nauseous, were their large protuberant eyes, ringed with what looked like heavy eyeliner. Worse still, they seemed to be grinning at the gruesome remains of the unfortunate man.

A cab pulled up, and the cabby rushed to Margaret's aid, ushering her into the back of his cab, then he called the police. The same cabby took off his coat and placed it over the corpse, and as he did so he too noticed the grisly trio, and could not understand why they were grinning at the tragedy. People began to congregate around the broken body, and when one of these bystanders asked one of the women what had happened, she said, with an inane grin on her face, 'He just burst when he hit the ground.'

'They usually die when their lungs collapse when they fall from that height,' added another of the morbid trio, craning back her head to look at the uppermost storeys of the block of flats.

'Or sometimes their spines crack and they die instantly,' said the third, 'but we saw one girl get up and the back of her head was hanging off, her all hair stuck to it, and her brains slid out.'

The person who had asked the question and the cabby looked at each other in disgust. When an ambulance turned up at the scene, the paramedics seemed to recognise the women, and one of them told them to get lost.

I also received an email from a worker at Lime Street station who had heard my broadcast. He said that in the 1980s a girl had jumped in front of a train at Lime Street and had been dragged some distance to her death, which was almost instantaneous, and three women had approached him on the platform to say they had seen the dead girl's shoes further down the track. These three women all wore scarves of the type described in the other encounters detailed here – and had tell-tale dark bulging eyes brimming with menace.

JASPER HECKLING

In the 1880s, Liverpool was visited several times by one of the strangest figures in the history of the supernatural – Spring-Heeled Jack – a man capable of leaping from pavement to rooftop and back, and up church steeples in a single bound. He was spotted right across the country, and was first seen in London around 1837. Spring-

Heeled Jack has been described as a Victorian Batman, dressed in a black tight-fitting costume, with large pointed ears and a long flowing black cloak. Sometimes he terrorised criminals, particularly burglars and grave-robbers, but he also had a tendency to assault young women who happened to be out after dusk, something the fictional Batman or any decent superhero would never do.

Now, to this day, no one knows who or what Spring-Heeled Jack was. Could he simply have been a collection of hoaxers and jokers playing pranks over the years, or was he a true eccentric – perhaps a mad scientist, years ahead of his time, who had somehow discovered a way to overcome gravity? Every time a baby lifts a spoon to its mouth, it is overcoming the entire gravitational pull of the earth. Gravity is one of the weakest forces in nature but also the most mysterious, and only now are huge corporations, as well as military organisations, pouring millions into gravity research. Many scientists have tried to patent anti-gravity motors over the years, and here in Liverpool in the 1960s, a self-taught man, John Stanley, gave a demonstration of his anti-gravity device at Central Hall by spinning 40 kg weights on a bar with an electric drill motor. As the weights spun round, a petite woman in the audience was able to lift them over her head because the centrifugal force had temporarily cancelled out the weight. Stanley also claimed he was building an anti-gravity engine into his mini, which would allow him to fly. He died before he could complete his work.

In 1881, a famous Liverpool police detective of his day, Alfred Lamothe, who lived in Plimsoll Street, Toxteth, actually investigated a man who was suspected of being Spring-Heeled Jack. It all started when the manager of the Shaftesbury Hotel, John W Lloyd, reported a burglary at his premises on Mount Pleasant at 9.30pm. The routine investigation into the burglary took a very curious turn when police discovered some suspicious items strewn about the room by the burglar, including a black shiny helmet of some sort, a hard red papier-maché mask of a horned Devil's face, a black leather costume, and a long black leather cloak lined with green silk. Straight away, Detective Lamothe thought about the recent sightings of the so-called

Spring-Heeled Jack in Aigburth and High Park Street, and so he waited until the hotel guest, who had signed into the Shaftesbury under the name Jasper Heckling, arrived in reception at 11pm.

Heckling was tall and debonair and spoke in a very refined voice. Detective Lamothe informed him of the break-in at his room, and straight away he looked very concerned, and asked what had been stolen. 'We're not sure yet, Mr Heckling, perhaps they took some valuables, you'll have to see for yourself. They didn't take that strange helmet and that devil mask and cloak of yours though,' he said wryly.

Heckling's face twitched, and he seemed stuck for words. 'Oh those wouldn't have been of any interest to a common thief, Mr Lamothe,' he finally managed to say.

'May I ask just *what* that helmet and devil mask is used for, sir?'

'Of course, I am planning to go to a fancy dress ball quite soon.'

'A fancy dress ball? And who are you going as, sir? *Springheel Jack?*'

Heckling was perspiring heavily now, and shook his head, 'No ... as Beelzebub ... the Devil. May I go to my room now, sir?'

The detective nodded and accompanied him to the room, noting how quickly the nimble-footed guest took the stairs, two at a time. Heckling claimed nothing had been taken from his room except a signet ring which had been of great sentimental value. Despite this, Lamothe said he would like to interview Heckling at the Detective Office on Dale Street at 10am in the morning, if it wasn't too much bother.

'Very well, officer,' Heckling nodded reluctantly.

'I just need you to fill us in regarding some details of a separate inquiry. We may be able to recover your ring.' Lamothe then took down Heckling's address, which was 72 Wine Street, Bristol. Outside the hotel, Lamothe ordered the police constable with him to go home, dress in civilian clothes and return to Mount Pleasant to keep watch on Mr Heckling if he should leave the hotel, but Jasper Heckling stayed put.

That night, Liverpool was covered in one of the worst fogs in living memory, and just after midnight, within a stone's throw of the

Detective Office on Dale Street, the silhouette of a man in an outstretched cape was seen to fall to the pavement from a nearby roof. Women of the night screamed, stray dogs barked at the figure, and before long, police whistles were screeching. One young policeman made the mistake of charging at Spring-Heeled Jack with his truncheon, but the leaping terror just laughed hysterically and somersaulted over him, swiping off his hat. He spat fire in the face of another policeman, and was chased for hundreds of yards towards William Brown Street, where he was seen by dozens of people. The fog worsened, and the police had to abandon their search for Spring-Heeled Jack.

The following day, the sharp-eyed driver of a hansom cab spotted something very odd at the top of Wellington's column on Lime Street. Perched on the huge head was a police helmet. Lamothe and a gang of constables stormed the Shaftesbury Hotel that morning, but Jasper Heckling had outwitted them again. They visited 72 Wine Street in Bristol, but no one by the name of Jasper Heckling had ever lived there. A week went by before the bellboy at the Shaftesbury Hotel twigged that Jasper Heckling was an anagram of Springheel Jack.

Gremlins

In the 1970s, an event took place that was not reported at the time for reasons that will soon become apparent. It was two days before Christmas, and late in the afternoon. The captain of an airliner, whom we shall call Mike, originally from Liverpool, was flying from London to New York, a distance of 3,470 miles. Almost halfway through this seven-hour journey, at a height of 35,000 feet, Mike started to feel light-headed, and realised he was coming down with something. He had been sniffling for most of the day, but kept shrugging it off as an allergy, but now he realised he was succumbing to the first stages of the flu. If he worsened in the next half-hour or so he would relinquish his command to his First Officer Steve. Anyway, 35,000 feet above the Atlantic, Mike heard a strange voice calling his name. He looked right, towards the First Officer Steve, thinking he'd heard the voice too; perhaps it was some stray radio transmission from a military plane in the area, but Steve didn't act as if he had seen anything. Then Mike heard the voice again, this time more urgent than before. 'Mike,' it said, 'you have to change course now!'

Then, beyond the cockpit window, Mike saw a strange, partially transparent figure. He looked away, perspiring heavily, convinced he was hallucinating with the onset of flu. He glanced back at the cockpit wind shield – it was still there. It had huge bulging eyes and large elongated pointed ears and was somehow perched on the nose-cone of the plane. Mike looked around the cockpit at the Flight Engineer, the First and Second Officers, a flight attendant and the purser. It was evident that none of them had noticed anything.

The being dictated how many degrees the plane should veer to the left to avoid a storm. Mike asked his Second Officer if there had been any storm warnings. None had been issued, and the Flight Engineer confirmed this. Mike then surprised everyone by veering off course, away from the Boeing 747's usual flight corridor. Mike had a difficult time explaining his actions, and knew he'd probably lose his job and end up under a psychiatrist if he admitted what had caused him to change course. Less than 20 minutes later, a localised storm, almost as powerful as a hurricane, swept by, shaking the plane slightly. No one knew what had caused the strong turbulence, but all agreed that if Mike hadn't veered to the left, the Boeing 747 would have hit it head on and been knocked for six, most probably with disastrous results.

Years after Mike had retired, an old airline pilot told him how he had seen what the old pilots called Gremlins in his cockpit; sometimes they even looked through the cockpit windows from outside in the rarefied air. Some of these ethereal beings were mischievous, others helpful, and they had been reported as early as the First World War, but no one believed the pilots' reports. When Charles Lindbergh made his historic solo flight across the Atlantic in 1927, he reported seeing weird partially-transparent figures in his cabin. Whenever he started to feel drowsy, these beings would encourage him to stay awake and even helped him to navigate. Lindbergh documented these Gremlins in his book, *The Spirit of St Louis*, and many pilots later wrote to him to say that they too had seen the same mystical beings. I wonder if any of the pilots flying out of John Lennon Airport have seen these so-called Gremlins, but even if they have, who would believe them?

The writer Roald Dahl is said to have invented the name 'Gremlin' in the 1940s. He was a flying ace and an intelligence agent in the Second World War.

SKIN

Around 1976, 18-year-old Liverpool Polytechnic student Judy Kendal visited the job centre that once existed on Leece Street, and while browsing the laminated cards advertising all sorts of underpaid part-time openings, she couldn't help but notice the handsome tall man standing six or seven feet away. This man, who was ten years older than her, was Mark Figgis, and when he happened to glance over at the young blonde, and his eyes met hers, he just knew in that instant, that there was something magical about her, and he did something he normally wouldn't do, as he was rather shy; he smiled and said, 'Seen anything you like yet?'

Half an hour later, Judy and Mark were in nearby Mount Street, where he bought her sandwiches and a bottle of Pepsi from the rather quaint-looking premises of 'Ye Olde Tuck Shop'. The couple retraced their steps up Pilgrim Street, talking about their lives and hopes, and unintentionally approached the Atticus bookshop. It transpired that the couple already had one common interest – books. After browsing through Atticus, which was filled with the mellifluous orchestral sounds of Radio 3, they went to Parry Books on Bold Street, where Mark, an unemployed plumber, praised Tressell's *Ragged Trousered Philanthropists*, and Judy perused a book on astrology, as she was well and truly into the Zodiac. From Bold Street, they went to a second-hand bookshop on Renshaw Street. The facade of this shop was painted black and it had a musky interior. Here, Judy found the book that was to cause so much trouble. It was an old silken handwritten hardback – in French – a language of which she had some knowledge. The book contained diagrams and tracts about 'resurrection stones', strange configurations of the Tarot, Hiramic magic, Thoth Hermes Trismegistus, and other obscure occult matters. Judy asked the woman running the shop how much it was, but she said it wasn't one of hers. She smiled, shrugged, then told Judy she could keep it.

Mark went to Judy's bedsit on Catharine Street where they shared a bottle of cheap red wine, ate Vesta beef curry and rice, and chatted into the early hours. They fell asleep on the couch, and when Judy awoke at about 1.20am, she smiled at the sight of Mark snoring beside her. Her smile abruptly faded when eyes met the dark piercing eyes of a madman in old-fashioned clothes who was leaning over her. In his hand was a knife smeared with fresh blood. Judy screamed and Mark woke with a start to catch a glimpse of the lunatic sprinting in silence out of the room and into the communal hallway.

'Don't go after him, he's got a knife!' gasped Judy as Mark catapulted himself off the sofa for the door, returning moments later shaking his head in disbelief. 'He just ... disappeared,' he said. The only other people in the flats were two old ladies, and they had long gone to bed and had had no visitors that night. There was no place for the oddly dressed intruder to hide, which made Judy so nervous, she asked Mark to stay the night, and being a true gentleman, he slept on the sofa.

The ghostly knifeman from some bygone age was encountered twice more. He appeared in the hallway of the bedsit three days after his first appearance, where Judy almost collided with him as she came into her bedsit – but luckily the figure vanished instantly – and then he was seen at Mark's house on Granby Street standing outside the bathroom as Judy was having a shower, and on both occasions that old book was present. Judy's father, who ran an antiques business in Chester, had the old handwritten book evaluated by a respected archivist, who told him that the work had been bound in human skin. 'Anthropodermic bibliopegy,' the archivist explained, 'quite rare but not unheard of. Anatomy texts were sometimes bound by the skin of hanged men, and there is a reference to a Maurice Gleeson Wilson in this French text. He is the man who murdered a woman and her two children and their maidservant in Toxteth in 1849. Quite a large area of his skin was used in the binding. 'That bump on the spine of the book was his nipple,' quipped the archivist with a glassy smile.

Wilson was indeed responsible for the so-called Leveson Street Massacre, which took place in March 1849. A 26-year-old Irish maniac named Maurice Gleeson Wilson battered and stabbed four people to death – Mrs Hinrichson, her two young children and her maid Miss Parr – at 20 Leveson Street (later renamed Grenville Street South because of the notoriety of its name). Wilson was subsequently captured, tried and hanged before 50,000 cheering spectators at Kirkdale Prison. I have written extensively about this heinous crime in my book *Murders of Merseyside*. The whereabouts of the macabre skin-bound book are currently unknown.

THE CROXTETH CAVALIER

Frank, who is featured in the following true story, is now in his seventies and happily retired, but he clearly remembers two nights, back in the summer of 1983, when he encountered an apparition that he and others nicknamed the Croxteth Cavalier. It all started in a semi-detached house in Woolfall Heath around teatime on Monday 29 August 1983, when 45-year-old Frank, his wife Michelle, and their daughters, 10-year-old Emma and 12-year-old Hayley were having their tea while watching the quiz show, *Blockbusters*, when the phone rang. Michelle had an idea it would be Frank's mother Phyllis and so she advised her husband not to answer it, but Frank left the table to take the call. 'Hiya, Mum,' he said, brightly, then listened for a few seconds before sighing. 'Okay, just let me finish my tea and I'll be right over. You'll be okay, just give me ten minutes and I'll be over.'

'What is it this time?' Michelle asked tetchily.

'She wants me to mow her back garden. She thinks she saw a rat.'

'Oh, Dad, shut up will you? I'm eating here!' said Hayley, grimacing at the idea of a rat.

'You sit down and have your tea, love,' Michelle told her anxious-looking husband. 'You've been working hard all day. You can do her flippin' lawn tomorrow.'

'Nah, you know what's like; she'll phone all night. She's just lonely. And to his daughters he said, 'Do you two fancy going to see your Nan with me later?'

Hayley's gaze never left Bob Holness on the television screen and from under her heavy eyelids Emma looked sheepishly at her fish pie. Michelle shook her head at the unenthusiastic response from the girls, and Frank sulkily rose from the table and went to get the keys to his van. Michelle kissed him in the hallway and watched him drive off, bound for the home of his pesky mother on Stonebridge Lane.

After Frank had mowed his mother's lawn, she gave him a bottle of white Barr lemonade and a plain arrowroot biscuit – just as she used to when he was a kid. He just smirked, shook his head, then sat talking with her in the back garden for a while. After about ten minutes, a rather curvaceous woman in her early fifties came to the adjoining fence and smiled at them. She was stunningly beautiful, and Frank's mum said, 'Hiya, Barbara. This is my Frank.' And Frank smiled and nodded as Barbara said hello. Fluttering her eyelashes, she then asked Frank if he knew anything about old petrol-driven lawnmowers, as hers had 'just conked out'.

Frank was a plumber by trade but had a smattering of mechanical knowledge, and in 20 minutes had fixed the rusty green lawnmower. Barbara then did something which shocked him. She pushed him against the side of her garden shed and kissed him hard.

'Stop it, I'm a married man,' Frank could barely utter the words, as Barbara's sex appeal was almost overwhelming. He staggered away as she gazed at him with smouldering, sultry eyes. 'I'm sorry,' Frank mumbled, stepping back over the fence. He said goodbye to his mum, and drove home in a daze with the smell Barbara's perfume on his clothes, and her lipstick still on his lips. He thought about the feeling he'd experienced as she had kissed him, and almost ran through a red light. 'Get a grip, Frank,' he whispered to himself. No matter how lovely Barbara was, he couldn't let his children and Michelle down. He wasn't that sort of person.

At 11.15pm Frank's doorbell rang, and Michelle could see something greenish through the front-door window, but she was in a diaphanous nightdress so she didn't fancy answering the door – especially at this time of night. She told Frank, who was brushing his teeth in the bathroom, that someone was at the front door. He gargled, came downstairs and opened the door to a man dressed like a cavalier pressing the doorbell with the tip of a thin sword-blade.

Frank swore and asked the man's name, and what he was playing at, and the weird night-caller muttered something that sounded like: 'Ya slubberdegullion! Leave the maiden alone or I'll run ye through!' And then lunged forward with the thin-bladed sword and stabbed Frank in his chest. Frank almost fainted, expecting to die, but he felt nothing but a faint tingling pain and an ice-cold sensation in his heart. The 'cavalier' then withdrew the sword, twirled his green cape as he spun round, and hurried off into the darkness. Michelle came downstairs, wearing a coat over her nightie. She'd heard the caller's strange voice and Frank told her what the 'loony' had said and what had happened. 'And who's this maiden you're to stay away from?' Michelle asked, eyeing him suspiciously. Frank shrugged, unable to say he suspected the costumed crackpot had been referring to Barbara. The cavalier appeared outside the house the next night, waving his sword at Frank and Michelle as they watched from the window. Many in the neighbourhood saw the apparition, and when Frank mentioned it to his mum, she told him she had seen the 'man with the big feather in his hat' in Barbara's garden next door on many occasions. 'She can't see him though, you see,' Phyllis explained, 'but I think he has a thing for her. He picks my roses sometimes and leaves them on her doorstep. He's a ghost.'

Frank went cold. From that day on he always went to his mum's house during the day, and always took Michelle with him, and he never again even looked at Barbara.

The cavalier is still occasionally seen in parts of Croxteth and some think he is somehow connected to Croxteth Hall.

SNOOP

Every word of the following story is true, but I have had to change some of the names and places because the people mentioned wish to remain anonymous. These incidents took place in 2009 at a small block of flats in Kirkby.

The dawn chorus was in full voice when 32-year-old Jane Nichols rose from her bed and pattered half asleep into the kitchen to slake her thirst. She lazily dragged a bottle of Evian from the fridge, unscrewed the cap which, as usual, had been over-tightened by her heavy-handed boyfriend Dean, and took a swig, eyes closed, picturing a freezing mountain stream. She put the bottle back, and through the window of the first-floor flat she saw the coppery tinged sky above the eastern horizon, and a morning star burning bright and steady within it. Jane's thoughts quickly turned back to the mundane world of finite time. She looked at the clock. It was almost 5am. Just three hours' sleep before the dreary cycle of work began again, and so she left the kitchen and headed down the narrow dark hallway back to the bedroom.

On the way she saw the flap of the letter-box open slightly on the front door. She guessed who it was: her nosy old neighbour Mr Hobbs. Jane was furious at this latest breach of her privacy, and this time she wasn't letting the old nosy parker get away with it. She hurried to the front door swearing, and undid the security chain. Then she slid back the bottom bolt, but by then she could hear the door across the hallway closing with a faint click. Despite being 80, Mr Hobbs had a knack of nimbly darting away whenever he was caught snooping. Jane opened the door and looked across the dismally carpeted communal hallway. She could hear the soft wheezing breath of the sinister old man close to the door, and she just knew he was watching her through his wide-angle door viewer. She could also smell the odour of stale urine he always left in his wake – the olfactory signature of the incontinent Mr Hobbs. Jane retched at the smell. She considered spitting on the glorified peephole, but instead gave the middle-finger gesture close to the fish-eye lens and then went back into her flat. Jane carefully slipped back into bed so as not to wake Dean, who was lying prostrate with his snoring face towards the drawn curtains. Just before Jane drifted off into the surreal layer of consciousness that exists between waking and deep sleep, a peculiar thought hit her: if Mr Hobbs died and became a ghost, he'd be an even worse snooper.

As usual, Jane awoke a couple of minutes before the eight o'clock alarm pulsated on her mobile, and she shared the shower with Dean, even though she wasn't in the mood. She'd gone off sex lately for some odd reason.

When she returned from work at 5.15pm, Dean was already home and told Jane something which chilled her to the bone on this sultry day in late summer. Mr Hobbs had collapsed and died that afternoon from a heart attack. His only daughter had broken the news to Dean just ten minutes ago. Like Jane, Dean hadn't been too fond of their snooping neighbour, but now was more concerned with the type of person the new neighbour would be. 'Wonder who'll get Hobbs's flat?' was all he kept saying, but Jane recalled the strange thought she'd had that morning. Had it been a premonition of her neighbour's death?

There was a row that evening. Dean wanted to go on a week's holiday to Portugal with his mate Merry (Meredith), but Jane asked him to wait until her week off was due and she'd join him. Dean said he just wanted a bit of freedom because he felt he and Jane were joined at the hip. 'Familiarity breeds contempt,' he told her, and she told him to get out of her flat. Dean left in a huff and said he'd be back soon for his stuff.

That evening, Jane sat listening to a Tori Amos album on her iPod, wallowing in self-pity and trying her utmost to drive any thoughts of Dean from her mind. She kept repenting all the things she'd said to him, and as she harvested these regrets, she sat cross-legged on the big leather armchair in which he usually sat. The only light in the room was from a cheap vermillion lamp shade and the soft muted glow from the plasma television.

A familiar but alarming smell reached Jane's nostrils, that odour of ammonia that was always present when Mr Hobbs was about. For a moment she forgot the old man had passed away, and then Jane shuddered. The smell was so strong, she had the feeling *he* was standing right behind her. In panic she leapt out of the armchair, and without looking back, walked out of the flat in her slippers and pyjamas. She left the front door ajar and went into the communal hallway. The two other tenants were both in their sixties, and although Jane had lived there for almost two years, she didn't even know their names. After convincing herself that she was being silly, and that there were no such things as ghosts, she went back into her flat and, to her relief, found that the pungent smell had gone.

Jane sat with the light on in every room and even put the radio on, as she flipped through all the television channels, shooting nervous glances around the room. She kept expecting old Mr Hobbs to appear, and despite the flat being ablaze with light, she had a recurrent feeling that her old prying neighbour was all too close. If only Dean were only here, she thought, fighting back tears.

At 12.30am the iPhone chimed as a text message was received out of the ether. It was from Dean. It simply said. 'I miss you x'.

Jane quickly texted him a reply, straight from her heart: 'Well come back then xxx'.

A few moments passed before the reply: 'I can't am in Wales.'

Jane rang him. 'Hello?' said Dean, and Jane knew just from that one word that he was upset.

'What're you doing in Wales?' she asked. The strong, controlled voice at odds with the tears in Jane's eyes.

'Dunno,' Dean admitted, 'just thought it'd be good to get away.' There was then an awkward pause. He couldn't say any more because he was too upset.

'Why do you want to get away?' Jane asked, looking at her engagement ring.

'Dunno,' Dean muttered. 'Just did. I'll come back.' He stood quite a distance from the tent of his friend Merry, so he couldn't be heard. He looked up into the clear sky above Clwyd, to the spectacle of the Milky Way, strewn like diamond dust across the coal-black face of eternity.

'When?' Another word and she'd have cried and destroyed the illusion of aloofness.

'Dunno,' Dean shrugged, sniffing back tears. 'Tomorrow maybe.'

'Okay.' Jane listened. She knew he was crying as well.

'See you later,' Dean said, and hung up.

That morning at 2am, Jane was sitting in bed, watching a DVD, when suddenly the bedroom door opened a few inches. Jane froze, hoping a draught was to blame. Then three fingers came round the door. Three old bony-looking fingers, with almost transparent skin, the nail of the forefinger yellowed with nicotine. And again that putrid smell was infiltrating the room. Jane screamed, jumped off the bed, and threw herself against the door, trapping the three fingers, crushing them between the door and the frame. Jane pushed with such force, the door closed with a muffled click, jamming the digits, which seemed to quiver for a moment before they somehow withdrew back behind the door, flattening as they did so.

Jane leaned against the door for what seemed an eternity, until the appalling aroma evaporated. She refused to move from that room until dawn, barricading herself in by pushing the double bed against the door. She tried to call Dean but kept getting a 'No Service' message on her mobile screen. 'You bastard!' She cursed the phone and held it high by the window but the signal strength bars remained a flat line. The reception at the flat was usually perfect, and Jane felt that the ghost of Mr Hobbs was somehow interfering with the iPhone's workings. She opened the window at one point and contemplated jumping down into the street below, but the drop was far too great for a girl who was just five feet three inches tall.

Just after four that eventful morning, the handle on the bedroom door slowly turned again, but when Jane screamed, the thing turning the handle released its grip and the handle flipped back to its usual horizontal position.

At 7am, Jane dared to leave the bedroom, and headed straight to her mother's home in Westvale, Kirkby. Her mum told her there were no such things as ghosts, and that her imagination had simply gotten the better of her because she was upset and lonely without Dean. Jane felt really offended by her attitude, and went to her old room upstairs and called Dean. She didn't tell him about the spooky goings on because she feared ridicule. Dean said he'd be back around 2pm, and that he no longer wanted to go on holiday with his mate. Just spending a night without her had been unbearable, he admitted, and Jane apologised for telling him to get out of the flat. She briefly returned to the flat to get ready for work and when she went into the kitchen, she was met by a sickening sight. Her used sanitary towels had been removed from the bin and scattered on the kitchen floor. Immediately Jane recalled an incident the previous February, where she had been putting a bundle of newspapers and magazines into a recycling bin and had caught Mr Hobbs red-handed, sifting through the refuse of her wheelie bin. In his hand he held several of her used sanitary towels. Jane quickly put the towels back in the bin and after a quick change of clothes, set off for work in a dreadful state.

Three days later in the darkened bedroom at around 4am, Jane awoke to find Dean stroking her face. His hands were cold. She smiled, but when she opened her eyes she made out Hobbs sitting on the bed. He reached out and touched her face. It had been his cold lifeless hand that had been stroking her face. Recoiling in shock, she sat up and to find that her old neighbour was stark naked. With a scream, she picked up a broken alarm clock and threw it at his head. She missed, and the clock hit the mirrored door of the tacky old pine wardrobe that Dean's mother had given them. Dean woke with a startled cry and switched on the bedside lamp but Hobbs vanished with the switching on of the light.

'What happened?' Dean said, as Jane seized him with both arms and hugged him crying uncontrollably.

'Mr Hobbs was sitting on the bed!' she managed.

Dean saw the clock on the floor and the crack in the wardrobe mirror. He swore at Jane, calling her lots of horrible names.

'He was there!' Jane insisted, pointing to where the naked apparition had sat moments before.

'You had a nightmare!' Dean bawled back, putting on his slippers and inspecting the damage. 'Me mam'll go mad.'

'It wasn't a nightmare ... he was here!' Jane got out of bed, and stood there, surveying the glass on the carpet, the alarm clock and its twisted black fingers, and the crack in the mirror.

'Hang on, what's that filthy smell?' Dean had detected the ghastly traceries of ammonia and stagnant urine.

'See? D'you believe me now?'

'Are you sure it isn't you?' Dean said, callously.

Enough was enough. Jane used every profanity, every swear word she knew as she let loose a tirade of well-aimed insults. She told him he was the worst lay she had ever had, that she had to think of someone else when they made love to get anything out of it, and that she wanted him out of her life for real this time. At five in the morning the taxi arrived and Dean left with two black bin-liners stuffed with his belongings. Jane spent a fitful night on the sofa, with the television on, and, as usual, rose just before eight for work. At her workplace in Knowsley, a colleague, 40-year-old Judith, lent a sympathetic ear to her friend's story. 'I'm not going mad or anything. My old neighbour's haunting me and I'm going to move.'

'No, don't move,' Judith advised, 'stand up to it. There's a man I know, I haven't talked to him for a while, who gets rid of things like this.'

'Get's rid of ghosts?'

'Yeah, like an exorcist. His name's Gareth. His mum used to work in here years ago.' Judith looked through the contacts list on her mobile and found Gareth's number. 'There was a woman, Mo Dycey, who had real long runs of bad luck; all sorts of weird things were happening to her, and Gareth said it was all down to a cursed marcasite brooch. He was right, and as soon as she got shut of it, the spooky goings-on stopped and all the bad luck stopped.'

'He sounds a bit dodgy to me,' said Jane shaking her head. 'I don't believe in mediums and all that shit.'

'No, he's not like that. Just give him a try,' Judith reassured her.

Jane looked worried, but seemed to be considering the idea, despite grave reservations. 'If he comes out to the flat to do whatever he does, will you come with him?'

'Course I will. Wonder if this is still his number?'

She phoned Gareth at lunch-time and told him a little about the goings on at the flat. Gareth said he was free on Wednesday and Thursday evenings and asked if he could talk to Jane. Judith handed her the mobile and Jane nervously answered a few questions. 'Have you got a faith at all in any religion?' was one question. Jane was an agnostic, sitting on the philosophical fence waiting to be convinced either way.

A voice on a phone can conjure up an image of the speaker in the mind of most people. Jane pictured a small blond bespectacled man of about 30, but when she met him she was surprised to find that he was just over six feet tall, about 40, with a shaven head that sported the shadow of a classic male balding pattern, and had dark penetrating eyes and a pointed beard peppered with grey hairs. He asked to be shown the places where the ghost had appeared, and there Gareth would close his eyes in silent contemplation for a while. After meditating on the eerie visitant in the bedroom, Gareth said: 'He's obsessed with you for some reason; that's the impression I receive. I feel that after his wife died, he became sexually frustrated, but didn't seek female company in the usual way.'

'Why doesn't he just go into the light or go to wherever the rest of the dead go?' Judith asked.

'He hates change,' Gareth replied, 'and although he'd meet his wife in the next world, he chooses to stay here. I'll have to try and send him on his way.'

'What's the next step then?' Jane wanted to know. She wasn't really that impressed with the exorcist so far.

'I'll need to stay here overnight in the hope of confronting him,' Gareth told her.

Jane was speechless. She certainly didn't want him staying over; she knew virtually nothing about him. 'Can I just have a word with Judith a moment?' Jane said to the ghost-hunter and pulled Judith by the elbow to the kitchen, where she asked if she could possibly stay as well, but Judith said that she couldn't. 'Stop worrying, Jane, you'll be fine. Gareth's a lovely fellah. Nothing untoward will happen.'

That evening at 10.30pm, Gareth arrived at the flat with a black Gladstone bag containing the tools of his strange trade. Jane made him a coffee and he told her to try and forget he was there, which was impossible, of course. Jane sat at the table in the corner, checking her emails on her laptop, but she couldn't stop glancing over at Gareth as he sat alert in an armchair, looking towards the living room door. 'Can you sense anything?' she eventually asked him.

Gareth nodded slightly. 'He knows I'm here, and he's a bit annoyed.'

'What will you do to stop him coming here?'

Gareth turned to her. His dark serious eyes made Jane feel uneasy, even from the far end of the room. 'Well, there are words I know, incantations. They've never failed me yet.'

'You serious?' Jane smiled.

'Deadly serious.'

'But what can words do?' Jane simply could not accept all this mumbo jumbo.

'Words have power,' Gareth told her. 'Words can start religions, wars, and destroy a person's reputation. Prayers are just words, and so are hypnotic commands. Never underestimate the power of words.'

'Will you be okay if I go to bed around midnight?' Jane asked her 'guest'. 'Only I have to be up for work at eight.'

'Of course; as I say, just pretend I'm not here.'

Jane closed her laptop and rose from the table. 'I've to get a bath first, and then if you want some supper just let me know, or you can just help yourself to whatever's in the kitchen.'

'No, I'm fine, Jane, you get your bath.'

Immersed in the bath, Jane began to wonder about Gareth. Was he married? He wore no wedding band. Was she attracted to him? He wasn't particularly good-looking but he did have amazing dark-brown eyes – or were they dark green? There was something about his attitude to his work that she liked. Did he like her though? Well, Jane usually knew in the first minute of meeting a man if he liked her or not, and Gareth didn't seem particularly interested in her.

In the middle of her thoughts, Jane smelt that horrible odour again and knew that Hobbs was near. She dropped the soap and remained stock-still. A hand was placed on her head, which made her go numb. In the wall tiles Jane could see a familiar figure reflected as he stood behind her. She leaned forward and turned around. What she saw would give her nightmares for years to come. There stood Hobbs, naked, with the lower part of his ethereal legs inside of the ledge of the bath. From the middle of his collar bone to a few inches below his navel, there was a long post-mortem scar, still stitched up. His eyes were full of evil and his skin was tinged with ochre.

Jane quickly leapt up out of the bath, sending frothy water everywhere. She slipped and fell towards the door, grabbing the handle with one hand to steady herself. She let out a scream and clutched at a large pink towel on the rail.

Gareth bounded down the hallway to the door shouting, 'Jane! What's the matter?'

Jane folded the towel around herself as the naked figure hovered closer. She undid the catch on the door and pulled it wide open. Gareth saw the ghost himself now, glaring at him with pure hatred. As Gareth stepped into the steamy bathroom, Jane flew past him into the bedroom, where she attempted to get dressed. She heard Gareth say, 'You have no business in the world of the living, Mr Hobbs.' She tried to telephone her mother, but the iPhone's signal strength flat-lined again – probably the work of the ghost.

Gareth could be heard reciting something that sounded like Latin, and then in English he suddenly called for Jane to fetch his bag. Jane brought it to him and felt faint and unsteady on her feet as she saw the contorted, twisted shape of her deceased neighbour's manifestation. He looked as if he was melting, like some waxwork figure in a blaze. 'Don't look at him! Get out of the flat!' Gareth cried, as he delved into the bag.

'I can't go out half naked!' she screamed back, holding the towel across her breasts. She backed away and Gareth removed a black book from the bag. He closed the bathroom door, as unearthly howls of pain echoed through the flat. Jane managed to get dressed, but chose not to leave the flat. She remained in the hallway, her eyes transfixed on the bathroom door, listening to the strange language of the brave exorcist. Gareth suddenly cried out in pain and swore. Jane had to go his aid. She yanked open the door to find the interior of the bathroom a complete black void of limitless space, inside which the apparition of Mr Hobbs was disintegrating. Bright coloured flames issued from him as he was melting away, bellowing at the top of his voice. Gareth was nowhere to be seen, and Jane was soon lost in the all-enveloping blackness. Icy hands with sharp nails grabbed at her, and she pushed them away. Agonised faces of green mist appeared out of the abyss and then dissolved again. Then a warm hand suddenly clutched at hers, and Jane found herself being guided back to the land of the living by Gareth. He closed the bathroom door and uttered the F word. 'They took my bag,' he said.

Who 'they' were was never revealed, but next day, over dinner at a restaurant, Gareth told Jane something that chilled her to the bone: 'Hobbs wanted to kill you so that you'd be with him for ever.'

Oh my god! And what were those hands that were grabbing me and why was it all dark in there?' she asked.

'I sent him to Hell, and that darkness was the upper planes of Hell. Those were the faces of the damned ... people who had committed murder. They languish for some time in that state, and then they meet a terrible fate.'

'What happens to them?'

'I prefer not to talk about this. It depresses me for days.'

'But he just seemed to melt,' Jane continued, refusing to take the hint.

'The minions were devouring his energy body,' Gareth revealed, and took a sip of his wine.

'The what?' Jane's morbid curiosity knew no bounds.

'Never mind,' said Gareth, checking the time on his mobile. 'I'll have to be going soon.'

'Someone else need your help?'

Gareth nodded.

'Can I come along?'

'No, I work alone ... I'm sorry.' Gareth gave a faint smirk.

'Please ... go on, I'll be your assistant,' Jane pleaded, 'I love this subject. I always have done.'

'Maybe,' Gareth decided.

MESSENGERS FROM BEYOND

When the elusive English summer sun in days gone by put in an appearance, people from all walks of life would arrive in grass-green Leyland Atlantean buses and settle happily down at the Pier Head for hours in rows on the benches overlooking the river, chatting to strangers, sipping long-vanished drinks like Zing orangeade, eating ice cream cornets, self-made sandwiches, and fried chips with fat that turned their newspaper wrapping into greasy tracing paper.

On this particular sun-baked July Saturday in the early 1970s, 32-year-old Maureen was enjoying her day off from the John Collier store on London Road, and she sat on a bench, relishing an Orange Maid ice lolly as she squinted at the white-gold sparkling sunlight reflecting off the Mersey waves. To her right on the long bench sat a dozen motley people, basking in the sunshine, and to Maureen's left at the end of the bench there was a single space, 14 inches wide, partly occupied by her slim envelope handbag and a twisted glass bottle of Coca Cola. She had to move these when a silver-haired man in a chocolate-brown corduroy suit halted near by and surveyed the seat and then her, with a begging smile. 'Ah, are you sure?' he asked in a soft Irish lilt.

'Yeah it's okay, sit here, go on,' was her warm reply.

'Aren't you hot with that scarf on?' The Irishman's hazel eyes surveyed the headscarf covering Maureen's head and tied under her chin.

'No, I'm okay,' she said, slightly annoyed at the man's suggestion.

'Take it off,' said the man in the corduroy suit.

Maureen gave a little hollow chuckle, and looked with embarrassment to the corpulent older lady beside her scoffing jelly babies, but that woman's eyes were closed in supreme appreciation of sugary bliss.

'It's a crime against aesthetics hiding hair like that,' the Irishman's nose now almost touched Maureen's cheek as he examined her fringe. 'That's Celtic hair. She's in the full bloom of youth, blessed with hair like an October sunset and she hides it under a rag,' he told the crying seagulls. There was a lull in the Blarney, and then he said something that stunned Maureen to the core. 'Anyway, to the crux of the matter; I've come to relay a few messages from your Aunt Sissy,' the man told her. Maureen thought it must some kind of sick joke, because Aunt Sissy had been dead for ten years. 'Yes, gone but not forgotten, Maureen,' said the Irishman, 'and she still loves you … you soft sausage.'

Aunt Sissy used to call Maureen 'soft sausage' when she was a child. *How does he know my name?* she thought. The eerie man continued: 'You'll have a baby on Sissy's birthday, August twelfth next year; a little girl. That's a promise. And just before this, in July, you'll be told to move house, so don't be spending all your hard-earned money on the place.'

With that, the man rose, walked to the back of the bench, and disappeared. Maureen asked the people sitting by her if they had seen him vanish, but none of them had even noticed anyone walk by. Maureen had been certified infertile by a doctor, yet she became pregnant and in the following year gave birth to a girl on 12 August. The month before the birth, the council said she would have to move out of her house because a new road was planned that would run through her neighbourhood.

The identity of the messenger from beyond is not known, and probably never will be, but such messengers are more common than you might think. One afternoon in 1978, 14-year-old Gerry from Walton, went to buy a Spanish acoustic guitar from Hessy's Music Centre at 62 Stanley Street in Liverpool city centre. The salesman told him to try the guitar he fancied first, and so Gerry sat on a combo amp and began to pick the chords to the old George Harrison song, *Here Comes the Sun*. 'You'd be better with a capo on the seventh fret with that,' said the salesman, and went to fetch the strap-on guitar capo while Gerry played the chord of D major. The salesman was suddenly distracted by a lady badgering him about a microphone she had just bought for her son, and while the customer and salesman were talking, Gerry heard a banjo playing the opening riff of *Here Comes the Sun*. A bespectacled man with long grey slicked back hair, stood, banjo in hand, with one foot on an amplifier. As he played, he smiled at the teenager, then suddenly stopped. 'Gerry, tell your mother not to go to Wales next week,' he said, then vanished. Gerry sat there on the amplifier, looking at the space where the banjo-player had been a few seconds ago, trying to take in what he had just witnessed. 'Sorry, here's the capo,' said the salesman, but Gerry didn't hear him at first. When the salesman said, 'You okay?' Gerry told him what he had just seen, and the salesman said he too had heard a banjo being played, but assumed it was one of the customers.

Gerry told his mother Karen what had happened, and what the banjo-playing ghost had said, and she went cold. She had been intending to drive to her cousin's house in Rhyl the following Friday – and realised that Gerry had described her cousin Graham Jones, who had died ten years ago. He wore glasses, and had gone prematurely grey at the age of 30. He always slicked back his hair. He played the banjo and guitar, and was never out of Hessy's and Rushworths buying instruments and songbooks.

On the Friday Gerry's mother was supposed to go to Wales, she was driving down Priory Road in Anfield, on the way home from her sister's, when her front right tyre suddenly burst. The car veered out of control for a while, and mounted the kerb, but luckily she somehow managed to steer the car back on to the road and bring it safely to a halt. Karen shuddered at the thought of what could have happened if that tyre had blown on the motorway to Wales.

THEY ARE HERE

In the autumn of 1979, 49-year-old former taxi-driver Stephen Hulme was evicted from his flat in Aigburth for drunken behaviour. He stayed at the YMCA in the city centre for a while, before finding accommodation in a one-bedroomed flat over a shop on Smithdown Road, with a fine view of Wavertree Playground, the vast park nicknamed 'The Mystery' by the locals. His drinking habit continued to blight his life, and like clockwork, each evening he'd go to the local off-licence, and buy a bottle of vodka and a four-pack of Guinness. By 10pm he would be staggering along Smithdown Road, on his way to various pubs in the area, bothering drinkers and making a spectacle of himself. Sometimes the people he irritated gave him a hiding, and sometimes the police would arrest him; but on rare occasions Hulme would go to a fish and chip shop and return home from an uneventful drunken night out with a curry.

One November night in 1979, Stephen hurried out of the Brook House on Smithdown Road after being punched in the eye by a student. He had branded the student 'a state scrounger' and deliberately knocked his drink over. He then went to the nearby chippie and almost caused another fracas when he asked an Irishman ordering a mixed grill if he happened to be in the IRA. At half-past midnight, Stephen Hulme finished his curry as he sat in an old but comfortable high-backed chair positioned in front of his rusty old two-bar electric fire. He then did a stupid thing that almost cost him his life. He took the last cigarette out of a box of ten players Number 6, and, finding he had no matches, took the silvery lining paper out of the cigarette box, rolled it up, and tried to ignite it from the bar of the electric fire. There was a loud crackle and a blue dazzling spark fizzed as the electricity was conducted by the silver paper. The current flew up the alcoholic's arm and knocked him out. When he came to, he was still sitting in his high-backed chair, with his head resting on its left wing. The fire was no longer on, because the meter had run out and needed another 50 pence piece. Stephen noticed a brightly coloured object shining into the room through the window panes, which were streaked with condensation. He heaved himself up and wiped the moisture with his hand. Outside, in the park, it looked as if the circus had come to town.

The park was lit up by something Stephen perceived as a mammoth big top circus tent, illuminated by blue and green lights. He opened the window, and immediately became aware of a very low humming sound. He recognised that sound as the one that had plagued him a few years back when he lived near Sefton Park. Many other people had heard the infuriating hum, and it had even got a mention in the local papers, but no one had been able to trace it.

Stephen left his flat and entered the park through a gap in the railings. As he got closer to the big top, he soon saw that it was not a tent at all, but something not of this world – a giant circular craft, about 150 feet in diameter, with a small dome on the top. Its hull was silvery-green, and there were glyphs which Stephen could not understand on one section of the metallic surface. Fearing for his life, he backed away from what was obviously a landed UFO, and hid behind the thick trunk of an old tree.

As he was wondering whether he should wait and see what would happen or make a dash for it out of the park, a door opened in the craft. A shadowy figure walked out. It was a woman, and when she was about 50 feet from the craft, its door closed and its lights went out. The craft then silently lifted off and Stephen tried to follow it with his eyes but it was too fast and in an instant it was lost in the starry sky. Stephen then watched the woman walk ghost-like through the park railings. She had dark collar-length hair, was around 5 feet 6 inches in height, and about 30 to 35 years of age. She walked across Smithdown Road, and down Crawford Avenue. Stephen decided to follow her and kept within about a hundred yards of her as she walked silently through the night. She eventually came to a house on Penny Lane, where she let herself in with a key. Stephen lingered there for about 15 minutes, then went home. He didn't get to sleep until about 4am, and when he awoke at 8.30am, he went to the park, hoping to find some tangible evidence of the huge UFO that had landed and taken off there last night. Surely, at the very least, there would be a circular impression left by the colossal craft? But there was no dent or any marking to be seen anywhere in the ground.

Around 11am, a group of men visited the park, and Stephen Hulme watched them from his flat window photographing the exact spot where the UFO had been, and he went out to get a closer look. The men were amateur ufologists (students of the UFO phenomenon) investigating reports of what they termed as a 'Close Encounter of the Second Kind' – the *landing of a UFO* in the park at around 2.30am. One of the ufologists held a Geiger counter, but was getting nothing from the ground. 'No radiation at all,' he said, with disappointment in his voice. A group of children gathered round the investigators, and then a man walking his dog stopped and cast an inquisitive eye on the operation. Stephen was just about to tell the investigators what he had seen that morning, when the woman from the UFO arrived on the scene. She was much prettier than he had imagined, with large expressive eyes.

In Stephen's mind, he heard a female voice pleading, *'Please* don't tell them.' He was stunned by the telepathic message, and looked at the woman in shock. He responded with two slight nods to indicate he wouldn't say a word, and she turned and walked away to the park gates. Stephen followed, and at the gates she turned and said, 'Thank you.' Her well-spoken accentless voice was identical to the soft female voice he had heard in his head. Then in Stephen's mind, he heard the woman say, 'Follow me.' She walked off, her posture straight as a plank as she marched, with her arms swinging slightly, and Stephen hurried after her. They went to Greenbank Park, and there she told him that she was from a planet light years away, and had been living on Earth for 60 years on a peaceful mission to study the human race. There were hundreds more like her on Earth, but her mission was at an end, and she was going home. The life span of her kind was about 1000 earth years, she explained. Stephen asked if he could go with her to her planet, as he had nothing to live for 'down here'. The woman's eyes filled with tears, as if she empathised with his desperation, and she studied him for a while, then told him his drink problem was due to a simple chemical imbalance in his brain. She promised she'd make him better in a week's time and that he'd be cured of his alcohol addiction for good.

'Will you take me with you?' Stephen asked again. The woman shook her head. 'What's your name?' he asked, and she said that in this world it was Mary. The couple walked out of the park, and at Hollybank Road, Mary told Stephen that most people wouldn't have been able to see the spaceship which landed in the park, only those who were psychic to a certain degree. He was about to ask more questions, when suddenly she vanished. He went to the house he'd seen Mary enter on Penny Lane, but it was empty and boarded up.

That night he kept an obsessive watch on the park, expecting to see the UFO again, but he saw nothing more than the odd fox crossing the green. With mounting worry, Stephen started to question whether he had imagined the spaceship and Mary, but a week later something odd took place. Stephen had spent most of his supplementary benefit (nowadays known as income support) and had resorted to begging for money so he could go for a drink. Having no success, Stephen went into a pub and ordered a pint of lager. As soon as the barmaid had placed the drink on the counter, he picked it up and walked out of the pub, gulping down the pint. The infuriated licensee, a tall thickset man, lifted the flap in the bar counter and came lunging after Stephen through the pub doorway. He wrenched the glass out of the drunk's hand, and pushed him to the pavement. 'Here, have this one on me!' he snarled, and threw the remainder of the lager into Stephen's face. Stephen crawled off on his hands and knees, crying. It had been a long time since he had shed tears, but this was the lowest he had ever been. He walked back to his flat and contemplated suicide.

He slumped in his usual chair, then the electricity suddenly ran out. He searched his pockets for a 50 pence piece, but all he had to his name was 32 pence. He sat and stared vacantly at the window as night descended on Wavertree. The elements of the streetlamps turned a vivid crimson as they came on automatically, and Stephen sank further into depression. He thought of Mary, and how she had promised to cure him. Was it just a hollow promise? he thought, and started to shake as the demonic urge to drink resurfaced. Desperate for a drink, he knew he'd have no choice but to resort to crime to quench his evil thirst. Premises would have to be robbed; people would have to be mugged, his need was that great.

In his mind, Stephen called out for Mary in the vain hope that his thoughts would somehow reach her. The response though, was quite unexpected. He was suddenly struck by paralysis and felt his eyes swivel upwards towards the ceiling. A point of light, the size of a bright star, appeared in the centre of Stephen's visual field, and it grew steadily in intensity until it was literally as bright as the sun, and gave off as much heat. What followed in Stephen's mind's eye was akin to a speeded-up film of his life, from the moment of conception to the point where he took to drink – a period that coincided with the loss of his wife after he discovered her affair with a friend. Stephen saw himself pull up at an off licence in Aigburth and buy two bottles of vodka, foolishly believing the drink would numb the pain in his heart. The scene changed to the point where he was drunk behind the wheel of his cab, and almost crashed into a crowd of children at a bus stop. He shuddered. This downward spiral into alcoholism made him feel ill. He watched in terror as he saw imaginary large black insects crawl slowly along his bedroom wall – symptoms of delirium tremens – the DTs. Those imaginary bugs would sometimes fall on him as he lay in bed, and he'd actually feel their icy legs crawling over him. The scenes from the day in his life when he found out that his wife was being unfaithful were played out over and over again until Stephen finally realised that he was not to blame and that he was better off without her.

Then he woke to a bright sunny morning, literally feeling as if he had been born again, and every time he thought of alcohol, he would recall the hallucinatory giant bugs crawling on his wall and feel ill. Stephen Hulme never touched alcohol again, and died in 2009, aged 79. Few people believed his story about the woman from another world, yet most people who knew him felt something had turned his life around in the autumn of 1979.

The Crying Girl

One sunny July afternoon in 1964, 25-year-old Vera Blackburn journeyed to Liverpool from Ormskirk to visit her sister Janet in Old Swan. As Vera left the train at Exchange Station a girl of about 18 or 19 approached her on the platform. Her striking elfin face and pointed chin was framed by raven-black hair styled in a straight-fringed bob. The teenager's vivid crimson lipstick contrasted sharply with her naturally flawless porcelain-white face and her eyes were ringed with heavy eyeliner and mascara. 'I'm so sorry,' she said to Vera, and began to cry, causing her mascara to trickle like black ink down her face. 'Sorry about what?' asked a baffled Vera, upon which the crying girl sniffled and said, 'Your sister.'

Vera froze, 'You don't even know me,' she snapped, then realised the girl was no more. There were gasps and yelps from the other people on the platform, because they too witnessed the girl actually vanish into thin air. When Vera got to the road where her sister lived, she was greeted by sombre-faced neighbours who were quick to tell her that Janet had died in her sleep and her husband – who was separated from her – had only discovered her an hour ago. Vera was treated for shock, and it wasn't until later that traumatic day that she found herself recalling the supernatural encounter at the train station.

A carbon copy encounter took place at Lewis's travel bureau just over a year later when a Mrs Hargreaves was browsing through a copy of a *Cosmos* holiday magazine. She heard a girl behind her crying and asked her if she was okay. On this occasion, the girl said nothing; she merely cried, red-eyed, rivulets of tear-diluted mascara cascading down her cheeks. There was something about the girl which gave Mrs Hargreaves a very uneasy feeling. The girl then vanished in plain view of several other people. An elderly woman with a speech impediment grabbed Mrs Hargreaves' arm as she was leaving the store and warned her that the girl was an omen of death. The old woman said that she herself had seen her twice before, and had afterwards lost a member of her family. That evening Mrs Hargreaves was watching television when her husband suddenly said, 'Bye, love,' and slumped forward in his armchair, dead from a massive coronary.

In June 2011, just after I had broadcast on my slot on the *Billy Butler Show*, Ann-Marie emailed me to say she had encountered the so-called Crying Girl at the old post office on Hanover Street in 1977 as well as just a few days before – gazing out of the second and third storey windows of the condemned Lewis's store. Many others have seen her there too. The last time she saw the girl, she had said, 'I'm sorry,' and Anne-Marie was involved in a car-crash that evening which almost left her for dead.

In the 1990s, a medium looked into this case and not only came up with a full name for the Crying Girl, but specified where she was buried. A fellow investigator kept a watch on the cemetery concerned and saw the girl's vaporous ghost rise up from its grave before solidifying and walking out on to the night-time streets. The medium stated that the girl had committed suicide around 1961 after dabbling in the occult 'with a group of very unsavoury people'. I asked what was unsavoury about them, and the psychic said they were an extreme group of occultists practising all sorts of Black Magic.

THE HATCHET MAN OF MYRTLE HOUSE

This story took place one lovely warm evening in July 1965, at around 7.30. *Emergency Ward 10* had just come on the television, and nine-year-old Jimmy, was having a game of war in the middle of a tenement block's square. The tenement was Myrtle House, between Edge Hill and Toxteth. As Jimmy was firing a make-believe machine gun and hurling imaginary hand grenades at his friend, his mother, Mrs Jones, leaned over the top landing and yodelled her son's name: '*Jimmy!*'

Jimmy shouted 'Oh, what now?'

'Hey, don't you "what now" me! Go on a message for your Dad!'

Mrs Jones held out her big muscular arm proffering a ten shilling note wrapped around a half a crown, which was in turn wrapped up in a list. Jimmy ran over and looked up, with his hands out, ready to catch the crumpled-up money, but someone had a huge white blanket hanging off a washing line three landings up, and as it flapped, Mrs Jones let go of the money and list and Jimmy lost sight of it.

'Where did it go, Mam?' he asked, looking about.

'There!' she pointed. 'Over by that grid.' Jimmy found the tiny bundle and unfolded it. He was a good reader for his age but this list had been written by his father, who was more comfortable writing out betting slips in block letters. The first item on the list read: '1 loave', and sugar was spelt 'shugger' and so on. Jimmy smirked at his dad's illiteracy.

'Hurry up, Jimmy, your Dad's going out after *Rawhide*!' Mrs Jones shouted.

'Mam, can I get meself some sweets?' Jimmy asked.

'Just a quarter, lad, and don't talk to any strangers.' His mother then squinted over at a woman she knew and saw she was with a man she'd never seen before, young enough to be her son. As she tutted at the couple, Jimmy ran off through the archway that led on to Crown Street, bound for the Cheap Shop – a store that serviced the local streets and tenements with bargain-price products. Jimmy however, with his butterfly mind, did not go straight there. Ten minutes later, he was riding round on a friend's scooter, and sharing a bottle of Jusoda. His father, looking over the landing, was furious and turned the air blue. 'Hey you, you dozy little so and so,' I could 'ave been there and back meself by now!'

Unperturbed, Jimmy ran off towards the shop singing an old Tommy Steele hit *A Handful of Songs* at the top of his voice. The western *Rawhide* finished at 8.55 and still there was no sign of Jimmy.

He'd been gone nearly an hour and a half. Mr Jones tried to calm his wife down, and his mother-in-law accused him of child-neglect and told him he should have gone to the shop himself. Instead of just going to the police, Mr Jones went round the neighbourhood, asking the children if they'd seen Jimmy.

'Yes, Mr Jones,' said a little girl named Carol with a plaster on one of the lenses of her specs, 'he was with some man by the fountain.'

The girl had no idea which direction Jimmy and the stranger had taken. All she knew was that the man had a hat on and a long coat. Mr Jones felt his stomach churn, and quickly contacted his four brothers across the area and they went out looking for Jimmy.

Jimmy, meanwhile, was walking along with a man he'd met by the Cheap Shop. The man wore a tweed trilby and a long greasy mackintosh, and had told Jimmy that he had 'loads of toys' for him. Jimmy said he was on a message (as we called errands in those days) for his mum, and she'd be wondering where he was, but the man grabbed Jimmy's hand and said, 'I know your mum ... we're cousins!' and he correctly gave the first names of Jimmy's parents, Jimmy's three sisters, and even the number of their flat.

Jimmy was led to a derelict old street (possibly Lonsdale Street), not far from St Nathaniel's Church, where the houses were scheduled for demolition. Not a soul lived on the street, which was near Lodge Lane. As Jimmy walked along with the stranger, he suddenly noticed that the man had a hole in the bottom of his coat, and protruding from a tear in the fabric was the corner of a *hatchet blade*. As the man walked along, the hole slowly gave way, and the hatchet's head dropped to the floor with a clatter, dangling by its handle. The man's big hairy fist gripped his hand and Jimmy felt weak. He couldn't even cry out. The man quickly picked up the hatchet and stuffed it inside his coat and dragged the trembling boy along with the power of a madman, saying through gritted teeth, 'Not far to go now, Jimmy!'

He pushed open a door to an old dark hallway with peeling wallpaper and damp mildewed plaster. There were holes in the floor and cobwebs everywhere. He pushed Jimmy into the parlour, and there on an old sofa, coated with dust, was a motley assortment of dolls – all undressed. The unbalanced man grinned brightly and said: 'Told you I had toys didn't I? You didn't believe me did you?'

Jimmy was whimpering by now. 'I want to go home,' he sobbed. 'I want me mam.' The man took the hatchet from his coat and gruffly shouted, 'Shut up! Be quiet!' and held it threateningly over the boy's head. 'I could put this blade through that part of yours he-he!' the man remarked, lining up the edge of the hatchet blade with the side-parting in Jimmy's hair.

'No, don't please!' Jimmy begged, his bottom lip quivering, wishing with all of his heart that he had not trusted the man.

The man then put one of the dolls on a low wooden coffee table, and lopped its head clean off with the hatchet. The head flew straight into the mound of grey and black ashes in the unlit fireplace, which made the man laugh out loud.

Jimmy was in floods of tears by now. 'I want me mam,' he cried.

'Whose turn is it next?' the madman asked, eyeing the row of dolls, then back at Jimmy yelling, 'You!'

He lunged at Jimmy and dragged him to the coffee table. Jimmy let out a scream, and suddenly, the parlour window was smashed in by a large terracotta-coloured brick. The frantic faces of Jimmy's Uncle David and another man peered into the parlour, and the hatchet man grunted with frustration, then ran out of the room and straight up the stairs, laughing like a madman.

There were heavy footfalls in the hallway as Uncle David and two policemen stormed the house. 'Jimmy! Are you alright, lad?' Uncle David asked, picking his nephew up from the table.

'He was gonna chop me 'ead off!' Jimmy shrieked, and began to whinge as his uncle held him tight, 'Ah, don't cry, lad, the copper's have got him now.'

'Up there!' said the older policeman to the younger one, and they both heard loud thumps upstairs. The first copper yelled out as his size-eleven boot went through the rotten stairway, and then the hand rail came away, and a shower of woodlice fell on his arm. The two constables eventually made it upstairs, followed by two more. But the rooms upstairs were empty. The police were baffled, because they could see the sole-prints in the dusty carpet where the child abductor had fled across the room to a corner – but beyond that there was no trace of him anywhere.

That hatchet man was seen all over Edge Hill and Toxteth for a while – and always went to ground near that empty house until it was demolished around 1970. One night, a few months after this eerie and terrifying incident, Mrs Jones and her daughters and neighbours were sitting up late on the landing outside their flats talking about the hatchet man and Jimmy's lucky escape – when suddenly there was a scream and a loud bang from Jimmy's bedroom. Jimmy was hysterical and when his mother pulled back the blankets he was in the foetal position, with a look of utter terror on his face. He said he had just seen the shadowy moonlit outline of the hatchet man in his room, next to the old wardrobe, barking at him to be quiet. Then a loud bang had sent Jimmy beneath the blankets.

'Oh, Jimmy, don't be daft, lad; how could he get in here?' Mrs Jones asked her quaking son. 'He couldn't get past us all outside for a start. You've had a nightmare, lad. You *were* eating cheese on toast before you went to bed. It's given you a bad dream, that's all.'

Then Mrs Jones's eldest daughter screamed. She had spotted a hatchet with a long black handle embedded in the side of Jimmy's wardrobe. It took four hands to pull that weird-looking hatchet out of the wardrobe; it must have been driven into the hard wood with tremendous force. It was taken into Jimmy's parents room and put away in an old chest in which Mr Jones kept his valuables. Mr Jones locked that chest, intending to take the hatchet to the police, first thing in the morning. The whole flat was meticulously searched in case someone had managed to get into the place, but besides that hatchet, there was nothing amiss. That night, Jimmy slept between his mum and dad, and woke several times in tears after experiencing realistic dreams of the hatchet man. In the morning, Mr Jones unlocked the chest – and found that the hatchet had vanished, and there was a sickly sweet musky smell in the chest that had never been there before.

To date, no one has discovered the identity of the hatchet man, and why this apparently real-life bogeyman returned to the world of the living to try and snatch (and possibly kill or harm) children.

Psychic Sandra

In 1977, 25-year-old Sandra from Netherley was walking down Childwall Valley Road on her way to her mum's with her two-year-old baby in his buggy, when she came upon a curious and terrifying sight. A group of people of all ages came running towards her. Children and women were screaming, and grown men with looks of horror on their faces were all rushing away from something in blind panic. For a moment, Sandra thought a madman with a knife or a gun was on the loose, and she crouched in front of her little son's pram, bracing herself. As the crowd rushed past her, she spotted a huge German shepherd dog racing towards her, and she assumed this was what the people were running away from, but the dog was also running away from something, and that something was the eerie figure of a man in a grey bloodstained suit. His arms were reaching out in front of him, and he was floating along about a foot off the ground. His face was streaked with blood and when he opened his mouth to make a loud groaning sound, his front teeth were missing.

Sandra knew instantly of course that the thing was a ghost. She had heard the rumours about the apparition that had been seen near Lee Manor Comprehensive for weeks, but now she realised those stories were true. The ghost flew right up to her, and she watched blood stream from both its eyes as it came out with a string of abuse. She even felt droplets of blood on her face and arms, but Sandra was so angry at the entity because her infant son was now crying hysterically and his little face had turned crimson.

'What the hell do you want?' she screamed at the ghost. The apparition's face twisted in surprise. It spat out several loose teeth and in Sandra's mind, the realistic phantom communicated to her that he had died in a car crash, and he was so angry at the way he looked now, because he had once been a very vain but handsome man. He said that as he lay dying in the car wreckage, he saw two young men grinning at him, and he swore he'd find them and kill them. Sandra somehow sensed, she had no idea how, that the crash had taken place on Belle Vale Road.

As Sandra stood there rocking her son, trying to calm him down, the crowd that had fled from the ghost of Lee Manor slowly started to creep back out of fascination. 'I don't know what to do,' the ghost told Sandra in desperation, and she wisely advised, 'Go to where you belong and be at peace. The ones who laughed at you will also die one day.'

At this the figure turned, and flew off towards Lee Park golf course, where it vanished into thin air. After that day the ghost never returned. Sandra though, started to worry. She had been seeing strange things recently that no one else could see.

In August of the following year, her parents took her on a holiday to Quebec, and one evening, the family went to see a cabaret act at a club. The first act was a magician calling himself Le Grand Melvin. As soon as he came on stage, Sandra knew that he would be dead within minutes, and she said the same to her parents. Then she went to the toilet and threw up because of what she had seen in her vision. The entertainer brought a seven-foot six-inch-long boa constrictor on stage, which began to coil itself around his neck. All of a sudden, as the magician was talking, the boa constrictor's powerful muscles flexed as it tightened its grip, and Melvin's face started to turn blue. At first everyone thought it was part of the act, but then they heard the bones in the magician's neck being crushed, and blood came spurting from his mouth.

The club's manager rushed on stage and taking hold of a ceremonial sword the magician had been using as a prop, cut the head clean off the boa constrictor. Tables and chairs overturned as horrified people panicked to get out of the club. A green and red gelatinous goo oozed out of the twisting body of the enormous headless snake and it squirmed off the stage and writhed its way towards the screaming audience. Alas, the brave manager's intervention came too late – the magician, Le Grand Melvin, was dead – and somehow Sandra had foreseen his bizarre end.

A few years later in August 1981, Sandra was returning from town when she saw a policeman being stabbed in the middle of Rodney Street. She ran to a Group 4 Security man who was walking to his van on Hardman Street, but when the guard ran to help, he could see no stabbed policeman or any sign of a violent attack. The guard called Sandra a 'divvy' and an attention seeker, but exactly a week later, there was a protest march by multitudes of people, many of them from Liverpool 8, who were demanding the removal of Chief Constable Ken Oxford from his position. As thousands of the protestors marched down Rodney Street, a young white man allegedly rushed out from the crowd and struck one of the policeman on duty. Not long afterwards the same policeman was stabbed in the abdomen, and was taken to the Royal Hospital. Thankfully he survived, but its strange how, yet again, Sandra seemed to foresee the stabbing a week before it happened.

Years after that, in November 1985, Sandra had a series of dreams in which she saw a coach overturning, and the Star of David symbol upon the tumbling vehicle. Days later, a coach carrying mostly Jewish ex-servicemen and women – most of them from the Childwall Synagogue – overturned on the A6. Two pensioners were killed.

But the most chilling premonition has not yet come to pass. Sandra foresaw a massive explosion in Liverpool city centre which threw cars into the air and demolished some buildings she couldn't recognise – until many years later. Those buildings have since been erected – down at Liverpool One ...

THE PROWLER

One Sunday evening in May 1941, at 11.30 pm, Mr Cunningham, a 55-year-old butcher, was returning home from Home Guard duty, and as he reached the junction of Hope Street and Blackburne Place, he heard a woman's screams and the sounds of someone running.

Although there was a blackout because of the recent heavy bombing by Hitler's Luftwaffe, a full moon shone over the city that Sunday evening, and by its light, Mr Cunningham saw a strange sight; a man in a top hat and flowing cape running at an incredible speed across Hope Street. In a few seconds he had vanished around the corner into Rice Street, and Mr Cunningham saw a woman of about 25 years of age, sobbing on the other side of the road. He instinctively went to her aid and she told him that the oddly-dressed man had followed her from her sister's home on Gambier Terrace. She had crossed Hope Street to get away from him but he had run after her, and seized her by the Art School where he forced kisses upon her face and neck and attempted to sexually assault her. The woman said her attacker's lips and hands had been ice-cold.

A policeman came upon the scene, and while he took a basic statement from the girl who had been attacked, Mr Cunningham went in search of the weirdly-attired assailant. He was armed with an old but reliable Webley service revolver, and intended to use it on the cowardly assailant if he resisted the citizen's arrest he intended to make, should he see him.

Around midnight, the gallant butcher was about to give up the search when he saw the caped attacker running away down Pilgrim Street at a phenomenal speed towards Upper Duke Street. Despite his weak chest he steadily gave chase. The man glanced back several times to present a very pale face, as if he was wearing theatrical make-up and his cloak billowed out as he ran into the darkness of St James's Cemetery, and here, Cunningham lost sight of the possible would-be rapist.

Nine years later, at around 10pm on the last day of May 1950, a full moon hung once again over Liverpool as a pale-faced prowler, dressed in a top hat and a long flowing opera-cloak, was seen by numerous people, looking through the letterbox of a certain house that faced St Bride's Church on Percy Street. On this occasion, something spectacular but grisly took place. The top-hatted peeping Tom was chased by the burly inhabitant of the house, and was run over by a car on Canning Street which seemed to crush the cloaked man's legs at the knees as he spun round under the vehicle. The motorist got out of his car in shock, and he and the man who had chased the spooky snooper, watched as the figure picked himself up off the road and dusted himself down, before racing off towards Catharine Street, where he vanished on Little St Bride Street.

A stranger with a chalk-white face, wearing the same type of long cloak and top hat, was encountered by a group of boys and girls outside the Rodney Youth Centre on Myrtle Street in the early 1960s, only on this occasion, he held the hands of two bemused teenaged girls and began singing and dancing and kicking his legs high in the air 'like Frankie Vaughan' according to the young witnesses. The kids thought the funnily-dressed man was just a harmless eccentric or someone messing about, until a couple of nurses from the nearby Children's Hospital came over to see what was going on. The high-jinks stopped immediately when the nurses came close, and the man startled everyone by running off at high speed, narrowly missing a double-decker bus. Two children mentioned that the stranger's hands had been ice-cold.

In the 1970s, police were called to Abercromby Park one night around 11pm, after several people had reported seeing a cloaked figure, perched on the domed roof of the Garden House, which stands in the centre of the park. The police naturally thought some student prank was at the root of the reports, but when two officers shone their torches into the park, they too saw a figure kitted out in top hat and cloak sitting on top of the Garden House. The policemen ordered him to get down, but he took no notice, so they climbed over the railings on the Oxford Street side of the park, and suddenly, the cloaked stranger casually jumped down from the Garden House roof and ran like the wind to the Cambridge Street side of Abercromby Park and leapt clean over the railings in a manner reminiscent of Spring-Heeled Jack. The policemen ran across Abercromby Park, climbed the railings into Cambridge Street, and saw the cloaked figure run at an impossible speed up Chatham Street. They chased him as far as Falkner Street, where he suddenly seemed to go to ground. The policemen did not for a minute think the figure was a ghost, just a particularly fit and agile young man, possibly a student, dressed in the type of odd clothes some students wear during Rag Week.

A few days after this incident, several drinkers coming out of the Carousel pub on Myrtle Street saw what was undoubtedly the same top-hatted man in a cloak, running at an incredible speed from Chatham Street into the car park of Sydney Jones Library, followed closely by a police car. The police vehicle turned into the car park, screeched to a halt, and two police officers got out and ran after the figure, who is said to have somehow scaled the 18-foot wall at the back of the Liverpool Girl's College on Grove Street. Police cars arrived on Grove Street, but somehow their quarry once again escaped capture, and was seen running off into the night near Sandon Street. Was this person a ghost or just some incredibly nimble prankster out to ridicule the police? The last report of this person whoever he is (or was) dates back to 1981. Maybe we've seen the last of him.

THE MAN WITH THE MOLTEN FACE

In the 1970s, a Birkenhead man set out late one night to visit his critically-ill mother, who lived in Kensington. He drove through the Queensway Tunnel, and when he emerged in Liverpool city centre, he instantly ran into a thick fog which made driving hazardous. Being in a hurry, the driver threw caution to the wind and accelerated through the streets, almost coming to grief several times, and was even pulled over by the police when he reached Brownlow Hill. Nevertheless, the motorist picked up speed once the police had cautioned him, and when he reached the district of Paddington, he took a wrong turn that cost him his life in a very horrific manner. Instead of turning left where Mount Vernon Road forks into Irvine Street and North View, the hasty driver continued straight on – into the oncoming traffic of a one-way street. He hit a lorry which smashed into his Ford Cortina and threw it over a hundred yards down the road, so it ended up on its side by Paddington Comprehensive School.

The motorist survived the crash, but was trapped in his crumpled car, which suddenly burst into flames. Horrified bystanders watched the man scream as the flames roasted him alive. His face bubbled and dripped like melted plastic, and he stared wide-eyed in horror at the reflection of his fiery death in the rear-view mirror, which hung close to his face. Two teenaged girls who were returning from their friend's house on Smithdown Lane observed the man's shocking death from close quarters, and suffered nightmares as a result for many years, and in those days, psychological counselling was largely unheard of for witnesses to traumatic incidents.

About a year after the accident, again in a fog, the ghostly image of the blackened, crumpled Cortina was seen by several people in the Paddington area one night around midnight. Then there were reports from people who said they had encountered the ghost of the car crash victim. One motorist waiting at the lights on West Derby Street, mere yards from the scene of the accident, said he saw the figure of a man in his nearside mirror, apparently walking between cars. He was like a blackened skeleton with melted clothes hanging off him, and his face was grossly disfigured, blackened and red-raw. The fog added to the uncanny atmosphere of the encounter, and the motorist became so scared when the ghost approached his vehicle, he jumped the traffic lights to get away.

Drinkers from the Mount Vernon also reported seeing the sickening phantom of the roasted car-crash victim one night, standing at the junction of Mason Street and Irvine Street. The man was holding his hands to his blackened face, which was hanging in shreds of fried red skin, and motorists who were morbidly curious enough to slow down to get a better look at the apparition, said the ghastly ghost's face contorted through a succession of weird expressions as they watched. Another witness, who passed the figure on foot, said she thought it was a living person who was bent over, apparently looking for something by Paddington Comprehensive, until she saw the terrible burn injuries on the figure's face and torso.

She ran off in shock when she realised it was the ghost she had heard her sister talking about a few nights before.

One evening in 1979, two drinkers leaving the Bear's Paw pub, not far from the fatal car smash, came across a man wandering in the road, groaning, with his shirt and trousers melted into his flesh, and smoke pouring from his upper back and the top of his head. The man's face was extensively burnt so that his features were barely discernible. The two drinkers went to the man's aid, and one of them said he'd phone for an ambulance, but the man suddenly started grinning, and his eyes were seen to light up. The drinkers soon sobered up and fled.

Sometimes, when it is foggy, they say that a phantom car horn is heard in the Paddington and Kensington area, always at the same time, around midnight, and some believe it is the horn of the ghostly car that crashed by the school all those years ago. If you're driving in the Paddington area tonight, do keep your eyes peeled, especially if it's foggy ...

I Saw What You Did

The following incident happened in Seattle in the United States in the early 1970s, and illustrates the often spooky nature of coincidence. I have included the story in this book because one of the girls, Carolyn Berry, was born in Liverpool, but moved to the United States with her Liverpool parents when she was seven.

One rainy Saturday night in July 1974, two 15-year-old girls, Diane Chester and Carolyn Berry, were babysitting at the home of the Keel family, as Mr and Mrs Keel were visiting relatives 20 miles out of town and weren't due back until two o'clock in the morning.

Diane was the mischievous one, and her friend Carolyn was always telling her to stop playing pranks on people. Around 9.30pm, Diane suddenly picked the phone up and dialled the number of a boy she liked at school. When he answered, Diane started breathing heavily down the phone, then said, 'I think you're the hottest, sexiest boy in my school and I want to make out with you right now. My name is Carolyn Berry,' then Diane hung up and fell about laughing.

Carolyn told her to act her age, and was very upset about the nuisance call. Diane apologised, then announced, 'I've got a really cool idea; we phone up someone at random and pretend we know some secret they're keeping. Everyone's got a skeleton in the cupboard. Shall we? Go on it'll be fun.'

'No,' said Carolyn, emphatically. 'It's an offence to misuse the telephone. Grow up and watch television or get into a book.' Then Carolyn turned her back on Diane and started twanging a guitar belonging to Mr Keel, but gave up after a few minutes and went into the kitchen and looked for some ice cream in the freezer. While she was in the kitchen she was annoyed to hear Diane messing about on the phone again. Carolyn ran into the living room and heard her say, 'Hello there, mister. I saw what you did the other night and it wasn't very nice.'

There was a pause at the other end of the phone, before the man asked, 'What do you want?'

Diane covered the mouthpiece and giggled, then continued her bluff, 'I want money, or I'll go to the cops.'

Suddenly the grandfather clock struck 10pm, and Diane started laughing. Carolyn rushed over to the phone and slammed her hand down on the receiver.

'Hey! What d'you do that for? You're a complete bore at times, Carolyn,' fumed Diane.

In moody silence the two girls then settled down to watch a movie. About 20 minutes later, the front doorbell rang. The girls exchanged anxious glances, because the Keel family had told them that no one would be calling that night. Diane went to the door and shouted, 'Who is it?'

At first there was no reply, but after a few tense moments, a voice answered, 'The police.'

Diane opened the door to find that it wasn't the police at all, but a big, overweight man in his fifties, with a shock of white hair. He barged into the house, pushing her backwards. She screamed and fell to the floor, and the man slammed the door behind him then bolted it. Carolyn scrambled to her feet and ran over to the phone and dialled 911 for the police, but the line was dead. The man had cut the phone wires outside. He then produced a gun and snarled, 'Sit down on the sofa!'

The girls sat there, trembling, clinging on to each other. Suddenly the man asked, 'What did you see?' The teenagers looked at him blankly. What was he talking about? 'Come on!' he shouted, 'You phoned me up and said you'd seen what I did! You tried to blackmail me ... didn't you?'

Diane realised with horror that her prank on the phone had backfired badly, and she quickly stuttered out an explanation: 'No ... no, sir, that was just me fooling about. I never saw you do anything, honestly.'

'Liar!' screamed the man, and now he pointed the gun directly at her, saying, 'I'm gonna count to five, and if you don't tell me what you saw and how you saw me, I'll blow your brains out! I'll do it! One ... two ...'

But I didn't see anything,' sobbed Diane, and Carolyn started crying too and then the baby upstairs started to howl, disturbed by all the shouting. Meanwhile, the crazy gunman continued counting: '... three ... four ...'

'I swear I don't know! I swear!' Diane pleaded, the tears steaming down her face.

'... five! Right, you're dead!' bawled the man, his gun still pointing at her, ready to pull the trigger.

Diane was so terror-stricken she wet herself, fully expecting him to shoot. But in a dramatic twist, the man suddenly put the gun in his pocket, then slumped into an armchair and began to sob, crying, 'I didn't mean to kill her. I just hit her, and she fell and knocked her head.' The man then became incoherent and buried his head in his hands, loud sobs wracking his body. Carolyn tiptoed over to the door and silently slid back the bolt. As soon as the door opened she ran for her life. The man still hadn't looked up, so Diane also seized the opportunity and ran out of the house too. The girls alerted the police, and soon the house was surrounded. The gunman didn't resist arrest, and calmly accompanied the police officers to a waiting squad car. It turned out that he had accidentally killed his wife a week before, after slapping her across the face during a heated argument. The woman had fallen and hit her head on a coffee table, and had died instantly. The man had put her body in a bag and driven to a refuse tip to dispose of it.

Then, by pure coincidence, young Diane had phoned him claiming she'd seen what he'd done and, by another pure fluke, the killer had heard the distinctive sound of a rare nineteenth-century grandfather clock chiming in the background as she spoke. The man recognised it at once, as he had mended that very same clock for the Keel family two months previously, and also knew the family quite well. He also knew that Mr and Mrs Keel would be out while their regular baby-sitters were in the house. There was yet another chilling coincidence; the murderer lived less than 100 yards from the Keels' home, and had even watched the silhouette of Diane talking to him on the phone that summer night.

Diane Chester never messed around with a telephone again, she had well and truly learnt her lesson.

WAITING FOR YOU BEHIND THE DOOR

The following story was related to me by several people many years ago, but this is the first time it has been published.

A carpenter was called in at first, because the door of the living room simply wouldn't stay closed at the rather average-looking terraced house on Walton's Lauriston Road in the 1960s. Philip, a single gay man, had moved there from his home in Norris Green after the death of his mother. He had nursed her in the final stages of a long terminal illness, and she had left the house to him after her death, but by then that house held so many bad memories for Philip, that he sold it and moved to a house that he had bought at a knockdown price in Lauriston Road, a rather quiet place in 1968, situated on the borders of Walton and Clubmoor – but now Philip was beginning to realise why the house had been sold to him at such a bargain price.

The carpenter seemed to have fixed the problem with the door. 'It was just the hinges,' he said, his huge broad hand on the handle of the door, which he moved back and forth as he talked, 'just out of whack they were. They have to be properly aligned you see, and I think whoever hung the door didn't really bother to do that.'

'How much do I owe you then?' Philip asked. He was tired and just wanted the carpenter to leave.

'Well I had to take the door off and re-hang it see ...' the workman began.

'Yes okay ... how much?' Philip asked, grumpily.

'Just a quid,' said the carpenter, though for some reason he couldn't look Philip in the eye, but Philip gave him what he wanted, and as the workman headed across the hallway, he sniffed the air and said, 'Mmm that smells nice. Your bird's perfume?'

Philip just shook his head, and opened the front door and stepped aside to let the odd-job man out. 'Bye now,' he said, and headed for his old Morris Minor Traveller.

Now that he came to think about it, Philip could also detect the sweet smell in the hall. It smelt like lavender or perhaps a cologne of some sort. Thinking no more about it, Philip went into the kitchen, made himself a simple boiled ham sandwich, then went into the living room, taking care to shut the door behind him, and then knelt in front of the black and white television. He turned the tuner knob, and BBC1 came into view. *Jackanory* was on that channel, so he turned to another station – Granada, where *The Sooty Show* was being transmitted. Philip didn't fancy watching that, so he turned over to BBC2, but that channel was currently off air. And so he switched off the set, got to his feet and noticed that the door to the living room had swung open again – wide open.

Annoyed, he put his sandwich down on the coffee table and closed the troublesome door. It clicked as it shut, and Philip's eyes ran around the frame, looking for anything that could account for the way it had opened on its own, but he could see nothing untoward. He was not a believer in the supernatural, but this was a bit uncanny and he felt a small shiver run through his body. Turning back to the coffee table he found that someone had taken a bite out of his sandwich. His stomach churned when he saw the bite mark, and he quickly left the room to throw the sandwich in the kitchen bin.

As he stood there in the kitchen, thinking about the door that refused to stay shut and the unseen thing that had taken a bite out his sandwich, Philip heard a thud in the hallway. The paper boy had delivered the *Liverpool Echo* a bit later than he normally did. Philip went to get the newspaper, and as he crossed the hallway the living room door started closing. There were no open windows in the house, so a draught wasn't responsible. The door closed with a click, and then Philip heard a series of loud knocks on the door, as if someone was kicking it repeatedly. Philip was now so filled with cold fear that he took his coat off the hook in the hallway, switched on the light, and then left the house, just to get away from what he now believed had to be some kind of ghost.

He walked down Lauriston Road, turned right into Grandison Road, and continued along Abingdon Road until he eventually came to Richard Kelly Drive, where he lingered for a while, wondering how long he could stay away from his home because of something he couldn't explain. Perhaps it was best to face up to whatever it was, he reasoned, and so he retraced his steps and returned home. Philip gingerly stepped inside his hallway, keeping his coat on in case he felt the need to leave in a hurry, and went into the living room. He switched on the television, then went into the kitchen and switched on the radio, just to fill the silent house with some reassuring background noise. It was now dark outside and Philip had the uncomfortable feeling that something was closing in on him. He felt that if he turned around, at any moment he might see someone standing there, and he had a strong sense that it would be a person of small stature, though he didn't know why he expected this.

He opened the kitchen door, which led to the backyard, and stood on his tiptoes for a moment, trying to see his neighbour's back garden. As he looked at their garden, which was faintly lit by the light from his neighbour's kitchen, he didn't feel quite so alone, and although it was cold in the kitchen with the door wide open, he left it that way whilst he cooked himself a basic bangers and mash meal. He sat down at a small dining table to have his tea half an hour later, and smiled as the children's programme *Hector's House* came on the television. He normally wouldn't have watched this programme but it too somehow made him feel less alone. He thought about the days when he was younger, when his meals were made by his beloved and much-missed mum, and how he would sit down with her and his father at the family table, feeling secure and loved.

After a few minutes, Philip got up to make himself a cup of tea, and when he returned from the kitchen the newsreader on his television screen had turned upside down. Philip knew that it was highly unlikely to be a transmission fault and just stood there, tea in hand, utterly perplexed, and unsure of what to do next. He fought against a mounting sense of fear, but his fear soon turned to anger at whatever unseen presence was behind all the stupid tricks. He felt entitled to some peace and comfort in his new home after all those months he had spent looking after his dying mother, and he found himself bellowing to the empty room, 'You won't drive me out of here, you idiot. I'm staying and that's that!'

For three days there were no further supernatural incidents at the house. Then, on the night of 1 November that year, Philip was rudely awakened by a series of bangs downstairs in the living room. He turned on his bedside lamp and looked at the alarm clock. The time was precisely one in the morning. Imagining there were burglars downstairs, he got out of bed, slid his feet into his slippers and grabbed a hefty brass candlestick from the dresser, then slowly opened his bedroom door. He stood and listened as five more loud bumps came from the living room. As he crept down the stairs the thudding sounds got louder and louder. He paused, lifting the candlestick in the air, ready to bring it down on the heads of any burglars, then slowly turned the handle of the living room door. He pushed against the door, but it hardly moved, as if something heavy was leaning against it, but the adrenalin flowing in Philip gave him extra strength, and he exerted even more pressure. The door suddenly swung open and Philip nearly fell into the room. Regaining his balance he reached round the doorframe and switched on the light, to be met by a frightening sight. In the mirror that was mounted on the wall opposite the door, was the reflection of something lurking behind the door. To his horror, Philip saw that it was a young man, of about 17 or 18, hanging by a wire which ran round his neck to a hook in the door. The youth wore a grey suit with wide trousers, and his hair was plastered down with oil and parted in the centre.

Then just as Philip was adjusting his eyes and brain to the image, it was gone.

He stood there for a few moments mouth wide open. With the candlestick cosh still in his raised fist, he looked from the mirror to the back of the door. An examination of the door revealed nothing, not even the hook that he had clearly seen.

That week, Philip was on his way to the shops to buy a loaf of bread and a pint of milk, when he was stopped in the street by an old man. He asked Philip if he was the one who had moved into 'that house' on Lauriston Road. 'What house is that?' Philip asked innocently, and the man gave the number of Philip's own house.

'Yes ... that's my house ... why do you ask?' Philip replied, and he just knew that the old man was going to reveal something unsavoury about the history of his house. And he was right.

'A lad hanged himself in that house,' said the old man. His eyes, magnified by the thick lenses of his glasses exaggerated the seriousness in them. 'He was one of them ... you know ... a nancy boy,' and the old pensioner waved his hand and pursed his lips just in case there was any ambiguity.

'What's his sexuality got to do with anything?' asked Philip, incensed at the old man's blatant bigotry.

'It's got a lot to do with it, lad,' replied the oldster, 'because his father wouldn't accept him. He disowned him because he was one of them ... you know ... and the lad hanged himself.'

'Where did he hang himself? Was it in the living room by any chance?' Philip asked nervously, putting aside the old man's narrow-minded view of homosexuality for a while.

'In the bathroom I heard,' said the old man, relishing the opportunity to spread a tasty bit of gossip. 'Used his own belt.'

'It wasn't the bathroom,' said a voice behind Philip. Philip whipped round to see a woman of about 40 standing there in an anorak, her nose rosy with the November cold. 'He hanged himself behind the door in the front parlour,' said this woman, 'and it wasn't a belt he used, it was wire off a lamp or something.'

'Well I heard it was the bathroom where he hung himself like,' repeated the old man weakly.

'Well, dad, you heard wrong, it was the parlour,' retorted the woman, and she smiled at Philip.

'I live there ... in the house where this happened,' Philip told her.

'Oh! I'm sorry, love. I didn't know ... I'm really sorry.'

'It's okay,' said Philip. 'When did all this happen anyway?'

'Oh, donkey years ago,' said the old man, and he nodded at his daughter: 'when she was just a baby, and she's ... how old are you now, love?'

'Thirty-seven,' replied the woman, and her face blushed till her cheeks matched the colour of her nose.

'You're more than that, our Ada,' said the woman's father, with his typical lack of tact. 'You're forty-two aren't you?'

'Dad, I have no idea when that lad killed himself,' said Ada, shaking her head in annoyance, yet smiling at Philip.

A white-haired man lingering nearby with his Jack Russell on a lead suddenly said, 'Are yous all talking about the fellah who hung himself on Lorry [meaning Lauriston Road]? I overheard yous like.' Ada and her father nodded at the dog-walker. 'Well, my 'arl fellah knew the family like, and he said it was in the late 1930s.'

'He hung himself in the bathroom didn't he?' Ada's father asked the stranger, who shook his head, yanked at his dog's lead and replied, 'Nah, he did himself in by hanging himself with a wire from a hook in the parlour door. He was only little you see, about five-foot two or something. He was a pansy – that was what I heard like; that's why he did himself in I think. When they cut him down he stunk of perfume. Why are yous all talking about him anyway?'

Saddened and disgusted by this dialogue, Philip walked away and headed back home. He'd heard quite enough for one day from the narrow-minded old men.

'Bye!' Ada shouted after Philip, but he seemed not to hear and walked disconsolately away.

That night, Philip drank a few glasses of wine to steady his nerves, and sat on his sofa staring at the door that had a habit of opening of its own volition. The television was switched off, as was the radio, and in the silence, Philip sat motionless trying to fathom the implications of what he had learned that day. He suddenly sat up, having noticed a partially filled-in hole at the top of the door where the hook had obviously been. Around midnight, that sweet smell he had detected days ago from the hallway once again filled his nostrils. Then he heard a voice, and at first he thought it was some passerby outside the window, but soon realised that it was coming from within the room. He strained to hear what was being said. It sounded like someone talking in a choked-up voice. He leaned forward; the voice was coming from near the window. He could just make out some of the words: 'Sick of living, but unwilling to die, you say I'm not your son and I'm living a lie …'

And then Philip was startled by the sound of a chair, or something similar, falling over, followed by violent thumping sounds on the door. He dropped his wineglass in fright, and watched as the ghostly, partially-transparent image of a young man materialised, suspended from the long-vanished hook on that door. His shoes kicked violently about, and his heels battered the door as ghastly choking sounds came from his throat. On the floor nearby, rolling on its side, was the stool the youth had stood on before kicking it away to meet his fate.

Philip rose from the sofa, and although he was terrified, he began to feel a great sympathy for the emotionally tortured phantom from the past. 'Your father did love you! Go to him! He loves you now!' Philip said to the apparition, and suddenly, the young man, who was very small in stature, stopped kicking, and his twisted face became placid and peaceful. He looked intently at Philip, and his whole body became solid for a few seconds. Philip could see the purple bruising around the teenager's neck where the wire had embedded itself into his throat and carotid artery. He had tears streaming from his eyes, but in a faint raspy voice he suddenly said to Philip, 'Thank you,' before closing his eyes gently, and smiling. The body of the apparition became limp in an instant – then faded away, along with the stool and the hook and the wire.

After that night, the ghost of the suicide never returned to haunt this world; Philip's words had obviously helped it to find peace.

I researched this case and discovered two old women from that area who knew what had happened on the night the young man died. He had been getting ready to go out to meet someone. He sat down and ate a sandwich, and then his lover turned up and announced that their affair must end. The lad took it very badly, and he sat down and wrote a suicide note, which began: 'I'm sick of living but unwilling to die …' He then obtained a length of wire from somewhere and stood on a stool, and hanged himself from the parlour door.

Homosexuality was hushed up in those times, and the lad's puritanical father moved out of the house immediately. Not long afterwards, neighbours would see a light come on in the front parlour of the house, and the recognisable silhouette of the teenager's ghost would be seen on the curtains, sitting at the window as he wrote down his last words. Then they would hear the frantic kicking sounds of his feet against that door – and the light in the room would then go off.

Ghostly Children of Liverpool

In the 1880s, Liverpool had the highest infant mortality rate in the civilised world. In 1887, for example, the grim statistics tell us that 46 out of every 100 children born in the city died before they reached twelve months of age. New York held the second worst record that year, with an infant mortality rate of 31 per cent. It is of no surprise to me then, when I hear of the many ghostly children haunting our city from Edwardian and Victorian times. Life was harsh and cruel in the days of Queen Victoria, not just for the destitute souls consigned to places like the Liverpool Workhouse (where the Metropolitan Cathedral now stands on Mount Pleasant) but also in the smoky, grimy factories, and even the schools, for life was even tough for those schoolchildren who were sent to educational establishments that catered for the middle classes.

At a certain well-known school in Liverpool which dates back to Victorian times, a very violent apparition has been seen, over and over again. The earliest report I have of this disturbing mirage from the past dates back to the late 1950s, when the school caretaker, a Mr Whittaker, was ready to lock up the building one December evening at 9.45pm, when the children and their parents had just left after a Christmas nativity play. Whittaker heard the faint screams of a child coming from the teacher's staff room, accompanied by the rhythmic sound of something being struck. The caretaker switched on the lights in the corridor and slowly headed for the staffroom, wondering what on earth was going on. Whittaker hesitated by the door to the room, then turned the handle and looked in. What he witnessed was both terrifying but puzzling.

The inside of the staffroom had been transformed into an old-fashioned room with oak-panelled walls and a huge mahogany desk in the centre. Seated in front of this desk, facing the caretaker, was an enormous bald-headed man with bulging, wild-looking eyes and a blotchy face. He had a pipe in his mouth, the smoke from which filled the room with a pale blue choking atmosphere. Daylight streamed in through this smoke from a stained glass window – even though it was almost 10pm on a winter's night. The obese fellow wore a yellow chequered suit, and stretched over his knee was a boy of about ten or eleven years of age, his head bent down towards the ground with his legs over the man's left shoulder. The bald man was thrashing the boy's behind with a long thin cane, and the young victim of this extreme corporal punishment was screaming and biting the man's white socks with such ferocity, they were blood-stained from the bites.

Whittaker was immediately aware that he was seeing some kind of eerie supernatural re-enactment from long ago, and he backed away from the doorway, closing it behind him, before hurrying down the corridor to the receding sounds of the whacking cane and the child's dreadful screams for mercy. The same disturbing sounds were heard at the school in January 1971, August 1980, and in October 2006 – and on this latter occasion, ghostly boys in school blazers were also seen running through a wall of the school and out into the playground.

On Mount Pleasant, close to the antiquarian bookshop Reid of Liverpool, a ghostly young barefooted girl in ragged clothes has been seen from time to time, searching for her mother. I once interviewed an elderly woman named Jean and her daughter Sarah, who encountered this ghost one rainy evening in 2003. Jean and Sarah had been shopping late (on a Thursday, when many of Liverpool's shops remain open till 8pm) and Sarah wanted to know when a certain play was being shown at the Everyman Theatre, so she and her mother walked up towards the Hope Street theatre, intending to afterwards hail a taxi to take them home to Gateacre. As the two women were passing the John Foster building (which faces the old former Irish Centre) they heard a child crying, and both turned to see a girl of about four or five years of age, dressed in a grey and black dress. The girl had no shoes on her feet, and her feet and lower legs were caked in grime. 'Mam!' the child shouted, and tears were rolling down her dirty face. The child's straggly, greasy hair was shoulder length, black, and looked as if it hadn't been washed or combed in a very long time.

'What are you doing out on your own?' Jean asked, full of

concern for the little mite, and she and her daughter closed in on the child, naturally thinking she was lost.

'I live over there. I don't know where me mammy is,' said the little girl, with unusually clear diction for her age. Sarah told me she thought the little girl had a slight Irish accent.

'Come here, pet,' said Jean, bending down to pick her up, 'I'll take you home.'

But the girl darted away, crossed the busy road, and ran at a surprisingly fast speed past the row of houses where the Feathers Hotel is sited. She crossed Pomona Street and Sarah was about 20 feet behind her when the girl suddenly slowed down by Terry's Barber shop, which is about 15 feet from the corner of Mount Pleasant and Clarence Street. Sarah then watched as the child ran down some steps into some cellar dwelling – but when Sarah reached the spot, there were no cellar steps there at all. Jean asked her where the child could have gone, and Sarah replied, 'Mum, I think that girl was a ghost.' For a few moments, both women stood nonplussed at the spot where Sarah had last seen the little ragamuffin, before hailing a taxi to take them home. The identity of the ghostly girl of Mount Pleasant, and why she looks for her 'mammy' remain a mystery, but many have seen her and are still seeing her today.

Not far from the last haunting stands Liverpool Community College's Arts Centre at number 9 Myrtle Street, which was opened in 1999. This building is one of the premier institutions in the northwest for those who would like to succeed in the spheres of Arts and Design, Fashion and Clothing, Media, Journalism and Photography, as well as the Performing Arts, for which there are courses in Music Tech and Theatre Tech. Three music students once told me how, during a practice session in room G20, they all saw the faint outline of a boy of about seven or eight years of age watching them from a corner. This boy and several other ghosts have been seen from time to time at the Arts Centre, including the ghost of a pretty girl with long ginger hair who runs about with a hobby horse.

In December 2004, several students heard the faint strains of children singing the Christmas carol *We Three Kings*, which was written back in 1857. I believe that all of the alleged ghostly goings-on at the Arts Centre might be attributable to the fact that the building stands on the ground once occupied by the Royal Liverpool Children's Hospital. I was a patient there myself, many years ago in my youth, and further back in time, around 1947, seven-year-old Richard Starkey, later to rise to world fame as Beatle Ringo Starr, spent six months in the Children's Hospital on Myrtle Street when he slipped into a coma after being admitted with a burst appendix. Just when Ringo was about to be discharged from the hospital, he fell out of bed and his scars reopened, and so he was unable to return to his much-missed home in the Dingle until he had recovered from this traumatic setback.

The first Children's Hospital on the site where the Arts Centre now stands was opened in 1866, and was demolished to make way for another which opened in 1907. This second hospital lasted until 1989, when it ceased to offer in-patient services. Many ghosts of children – as well as phantom nurses – were reported at the hospital, and I have a whole book of reports of such supernatural phenomena dating back to the early 1960s, so I am not surprised at the present-day reports of alleged paranormal incidents at the Arts Centre.

On many occasions since at least the 1960s, scores of people have seen three ghostly boys in school caps, blazers and short trousers, pedalling on rather old fashioned-bikes across Wavertree Park (which is known as the 'Mystery' by locals). These three children look solid enough at first, but after travelling about a hundred feet or so across the park, they vanish into thin air. Some believe the apparitions are of three boys who were knocked down and killed on their bikes on nearby Prince Alfred Road many years ago, but I have not to date found any records of such a triple death on that road. One person who saw the ghostly cyclists close up said they seemed oblivious to him as they rode their bikes across the park, near to the Wavertree Athletic Centre. The witness recalled that bike sheds had once stood at the location where he had seen the ghosts, back in the 1950s, and he feels the cyclists were not the result of some tragedy but merely a recurring timeslip.

In 2009, 55-year-old Martin from West Derby came down with a bad case of 'flu, and the doctor advised him to stay in bed, but Martin was not the type who could sit still for long, and he tried to sneak downstairs to finish painting his hallway, but his wife Jacqui took him by the arm and led him straight back to the bedroom, saying, 'You're to rest in bed until you're better. You're not sniffling about down here spreading your germs all over us.'

Once he felt a bit better, Martin read book after book in an effort to kill the boredom, and then he went mooching through an old suitcase he'd had since his early twenties that had been sitting on top of the wardrobe for years gathering dust. He found a slim 60-page volume on ornithology that had been given to him by his dad when he was a kid; the *Ladybird Book of British Birds and their Nests*. Then came the second surprise: covered in dust in a corner of the suitcase was a pair of Dollond & Aitchison binoculars that he had borrowed from his late uncle nearly 20 years ago. He took the binoculars from their orange-brown case and went to the window to try them out. Martin's house was situated on Finch Lane, and overlooked Yew Tree Cemetery. He focused on the array of white, black and grey headstones which faded into the misty distance on this gloomy afternoon, and he suddenly noticed something quite odd, and rather distressing.

Lying on one of the graves was a child – a little boy in a brown suit with blonde hair, with his arm curled around his head, apparently face-down in the grass covering the grave. Martin watched for a while, and then went to the top of the stairs and shouted to his wife Jacqui. 'What now?' she replied tetchily.

'Come and have a look at this!' Martin shouted, leaning over the banister.

'You're supposed to be in bed, Martin,' she shouted from the bottom of the stairs. 'You're never going to get better at this rate.'

'Just come up and look at this, it's really odd!' Martin shouted, and his wife reluctantly came up the stairs, complaining that she had a lot of housework to get through. She went to the window with Martin and he handed her the binoculars and pointed to the brown spot in the distance.

'What am I supposed to be looking for?' she asked, adjusting the eyepieces of the old binoculars to her eyes. After a few seconds she said, 'Is that a kid over there? How do you focus this thing properly?'

'So you can see it? I thought I was seeing things,' said Martin with a look of mild relief in his watery eyes. 'Just turn that wheel thingy in the middle there,' he said, pointing to the focusing thumbwheel of the binoculars.

Jacqui turned the wheel, and then lowered the binoculars and said, 'He isn't with anyone, poor little thing. Ah, he must be lost. I'd better go and check he's okay.'

'I'll go with you, come on,' said Martin, eager to get out of the stuffy bedroom.

'Any excuse not to stay in bed, eh?'

Wife and husband went downstairs and put on their coats, leaving their teenaged sons in the house. They hurried into Yewtree Cemetery where they searched and searched, but there was no sign of the boy in the brown suit. They even asked several people visiting the graves of loved ones, but no one had seen any fair-haired child in a brown suit. Reluctantly, Jacqui and Martin returned to their home on Finch Lane. After Jacqui had made her husband another Lemsip, he went upstairs to take another look out of the bedroom window with his binoculars. He saw just two people in the distance in the cemetery, and then about ten minutes afterwards, he saw the child in brown again, lying prostrate on the same grave. Martin went to the door and shouted down into the hallway: 'Jacqui! Jacqui! He's back again!'

The sound of a pan being dropped in the sink and some muttered swearing followed by, 'God! Wait a mo, will you!' finally brought Jacqui back up the stairs. Husband and wife went to the window, and this time Jacqui was able to get a good look at the mysterious boy. 'I'm phoning the police,' she decided, and looked around for Martin's mobile.

'No, wait, we could get done for wasting police time,' argued a worried-looking Martin. 'He might go missing again and then they'd say we made it up.'

'He won't, he's still there ...' Jacqui was saying, when suddenly she saw that the boy *wasn't there* anymore. She squinted her eyes and adjusted the thumbwheel as she tried to get to grips with what was going on. Her instincts told her that boy they had seen was a ghost. Nothing made sense otherwise. Then she saw him appear out of thin air, this time in a standing position by the gravestone on which he kept prostrating himself. 'Oh! He's back again! Oh my God! he just ... appeared!' Jacqui was too afraid to carry on looking through the binoculars, but Martin persuaded her to share the left eyepiece while he looked through the right, and he and his wife both gasped in unison when the child sunk to his knees, fell forward, face-down – and then vanished as though the earth had swallowed him up.

The skies seemed to darken by the minute, and suddenly there was a heavy downpour. 'I'm drawing the curtains,' Jacqui said and she pulled the curtains together. Martin tried to peep through them but she grabbed his hand and looked him sternly in the eyes. 'It's a ghost,' she said, brooking no argument and after an eerie pause of taut silence, added, 'Maybe we should pray for him, whoever the poor thing is.'

'Let's just have one more look,' said a curious Martin, sneezing into a tissue.

'No,' Jacqui told him firmly, 'I don't think the living should have anything to do with spirits and the dead; no good can come of it.'

'Alright,' sighed Martin. Jacqui traditionally wore the trousers in their house and he usually knew when to admit defeat for the sake of peace and harmony, 'Think I'll try and have a sleep.' He lay back on the bed fully intending to have another peep as soon as she was safely back downstairs

Jacqui eyed him suspiciously. 'Martin, if you love and respect me, you won't look out at that ... thing ... again. Promise me you won't look?'

'I promise, I promise,' sighed Martin, but as soon as Jacqui was safely out of the way, he was at the window – but his wife expected him to do exactly that and quietly opened the door and said, 'And you promised me ...'

Martin turned, startled, and said, 'No, erm ... I'm just letting a wasp out ...' but before he could continue to elaborate upon his lie, Jacqui shot a look of deep disappointment at him, then left the bedroom, slamming the door shut as she went.

'You're always telling me what I can and can't do! I'm sick of it! Control freak!' Martin shouted at the door, and he heard the faint profanity that was his wife's reply as she descended the stairs in a huff.

Martin defiantly went back to the window and looked out. It was raining heavily now, and the cemetery was devoid of any activity. There was no sign of the boy, even though he kept watch for about 15 minutes, then sat back on his bed, leafing through his old Ladybird book of ornithology, and eventually dozed off.

When Martin awoke the room was in darkness. He had forgotten all about the sinister figure of the child in Yewtree Cemetery until he saw that the curtains were drawn. He got to his feet, feeling stuffy and groggy because of the flu, and pulled the curtains back. Finch Lane was bathed in the usual orange light of the sodium street lamps, and now the cemetery beyond was barely visible. Martin went downstairs to be greeted with, 'you should have stayed in bed,' but he shook his head, coughed, and said he was sick of looking at the bedroom; it was depressing. He watched the telly for a while, and then, around half-past nine, Jacqui coaxed him back up to the bedroom and brought a portable television with an inbuilt DVD player up to the room. 'Why don't you watch *The Shawshank Redemption*, you like that.' And Jacqui looked for the film in question in Martin's collection of DVDs.

'Nah, I'm not in the mood for that. I'll think of something to pass the time,' Martin told her, and decided to read something instead. He asked Jacqui to go into the spare room and fetch a bundle of his old Marvel comics. He needed something light to read, and those old comic books usually did the trick. Jacqui brought the bundles of the old 1970s glossy-covered comics into the room minutes later, then left the customary bottle of Lucozade at her husband's bedside, kissed his cheek, and went downstairs to make some greeting cards, as Jacqui had a craft area in the living room where she liked to indulge in her hobby.

A quarter of an hour passed, and as Martin read about the comic-strip adventures of Thor and his dynamic battles with Loki, he thought he heard a tapping sound. He looked around and listened. He could hear the faint music from the television downstairs. Then, there it was again – and this time Martin gauged that it was coming from the window. It sounded like the gentle tapping of a moth against the window pane. He opened the curtains.

A child with vivid flaxen hair and dark, mad-looking eyes, was floating outside the window with his palms resting against the window panes. Martin shot back in terror, and without managing to utter a single syllable of surprise, he turned and ran out of the room, and only when he was halfway down the stairs, did he regain the power of speech, but even before he shouted, his wife had heard the heavy thumping on the stairs. She quickly rose from her armchair and ran into the hall.

'Jacqui! He's at the window!' Martin yelled, almost colliding with his wife in the hallway.

'Who is?' Jacqui asked, but then she suddenly realised with horror, who her husband was talking about, for that child in brown she had seen in the cemetery had played on her mind all day.

'That boy! He's at the window; he looked horrible. Jesus Christ!' shuddered Martin, starting to hyperventilate.

'Are you sure you weren't asleep?' asked Jacqui, struggling to explain the eerie situation away. 'It wasn't a nightmare was it?'

Martin swore at her – something he hadn't done to her face in a long long time. 'It's haunting us, you bloody fool!'

Just then they both heard faint footsteps upstairs, and both looked up at the ceiling. Martin hoped and prayed that it was just one of their sons, but when he asked if they were in, Jacqui shook her head and looked at the ceiling in wide-eyed terror.

The couple remained huddled together in that living room till 11.30pm, when their two sons, Dean and Tom, returned from the local pub. They thought their parents were barmy, and checked all the upstairs rooms to find nothing amiss, but when Martin and Jacqui went up to their bedroom, they noticed the small tell-tale handprints on the *outside* of the window, and shuddered.

A friend of the family got in touch with a priest – who refused to bless the house because he didn't believe in ghosts (even though they are mentioned in the Bible along with unclean spirits) – and so a medium was eventually contacted. This woman was not a 'professional' showbizzy charlatan of the kind which seem to be proliferating nowadays, but a down-to-earth woman in her sixties who did not even charge for her services. She said that the child seen in Yewtree Cemetery had been unable to accept his mother's death, which had taken place around the early 20th century. The boy would continually run away from home to visit the cemetery where he would lie on the grave of his beloved mother, sobbing inconsolably.

There was also a very unnerving coincidence connected to this case, according to the psychic; the boy had once lived at the very house where Martin and Jacqui now lived, and he had died there when he was still quite young from some fever. The psychic 'cleansed the house' and lit several white candles in all the rooms, and after this ritual, the boy was seen no more – and Martin never dared to look at Yewtree Cemetery through those binoculars again.

Turn Back the Clock

In the 1980s, 30-year-old Catherine from Crosby took her own life. She discovered that her husband, Lewis, whom she had loved since she was a schoolgirl, had been seeing another woman behind her back, and that things between Lewis and the other woman (whose name was Vanessa) were getting very serious. Lewis had angrily denied that he was having an affair at first, but then, plagued with guilt, and realising he should have stayed with his wife because he really did love her, he decided to end his relationship with Vanessa, who was ten years his junior, and return at once to Catherine. He planned to apologise to Catherine and take her to Paris for the weekend, but when he got home on that December night in 1986, he was greeted first by the choking, salty smell of gas and then he came upon her kneeling in front of the cooker with her head in the gas oven. She'd drunk half a bottle of vodka before going through with the suicide, maybe to obtain Dutch courage, or simply to kill the pain she must have felt in her broken heart at the ultimate betrayal. She'd choked on her own vomit.

Lewis never got over it her death and each evening he would sit and watch television, unable to take in what he was watching, because his guilt-riddled mind was always elsewhere. He never looked at another woman in the way he used to look at his beloved Catherine and never motivated himself to socialise again after that traumatic night. No woman could ever replace Catherine, and the lonely years dragged by.

In late November 1997, Lewis went to his local supermarket one afternoon, and was surprised to meet an old friend from university, a handsome Indian man named Madhav, who was now working as a software developer. Madhav was a wizard with computers and simultaneously read dictionaries of mathematics, electronics and physics in days. Madhav said he had heard about Lewis's tragic loss a few years back while he was working in London, and had been shocked and saddened by it. He had only met Catherine twice but she had struck him as a lovely genuine person. Seeing how depressed his old friend was, Madhav said he'd come round sometime and see him, and Lewis said he'd like that. Lewis had five main friends, and all of them had offered to take him out for a drink, but he had always refused, because he couldn't bring himself to visit the places he and his lost love had frequented in Liverpool city centre, they all brought back so many painful memories of happier times.

Madhav came around two nights later, and although he didn't drink, he brought Lewis an expensive bottle of wine – a New Zealand chardonnay – and a 1982 copy of *Wisden's Cricketers' Almanac* – which Madhav had borrowed from him six years back. 'Ah, you remembered at last!' said Lewis with delight, upon seeing his old book.

The two men talked into the night, and at around half-past midnight, Lewis fell silent. He stared at the floor with a contemplative expression, and said: 'Do you remember that time when we were in that cafe on Bold Street – about five or six years ago now, so I don't really expect you to remember – but you had a theory about time travel? You said you were going to carry out an experiment to test your theory.'

Madhav smiled, and his huge expressive eyes looked up to the ceiling. 'Wow – you have got a great memory, Lew; yes I remember.' And he gave a chuckle. 'I never did get round to trying out the experiment. We weren't afraid to think way out in those days, were we?'

'No,' said Lewis, and he swirled his white wine around in the glass, sipped some of it, and then squeezed one eye shut as he awkwardly pitched an odd question at Madhav. 'Is it possible? I mean if anyone cracked time travel it'd be you wouldn't it?'

Madhav folded his arms and relaxed back into the armchair. He thought before he spoke; he thought deeply, as was his way with all areas of the hypothetical. 'I'm not sure, Lew, but ... well ... okay, my theory was that, it might be possible to bring the past back through resonation.'

'Okay, you lost me in the first sentence,' Lewis admitted.

'Alright, well you know what sympathy and resonance is?' Madhav asked. He pointed at Lewis's acoustic guitar resting in the corner of the room, 'If I generated a sound wave with a frequency of 440 Hertz, then the A and E strings on that guitar would make a sound as if you had gently picked them, because those two strings are tuned to that frequency. Or, if you wet the tip of your index finger and rub it in a circular motion around the rim of that wine glass you are holding, it'll make a ringing sound – that's resonance as well.'

'Yes, but what's all this got to do with time travel?' Lewis was eager to know.

'Well,' Madhav leaned forward on the edge of the armchair's soft leather seat, 'I believe that if you recreated a certain situation from the past; perhaps reconstructing the scenario in detail of some event that happened long ago, then every element would resonate with the original event and perhaps – just perhaps – open up the past. It's just a theory.'

After considering this theory for just a few moments with a mind relaxed by the wine, Lewis speculated: 'Maybe your theory could explain déjà vu – when we think we know what's going to happen next, and it often does, and we can't explain it.'

Madhav shrugged. 'It's possible – perhaps all the elements have come together in the pattern they originally formed some time ago, and somehow reversed time, and talking of time ... I better be on my way.'

'Do you realise what day it is this Friday?' Lewis asked, with a doleful look, straight into the eyes of his friend.

Madhav had an idea what day his friend was referring to but didn't like to say. He simply said nothing.

Lewis forced a smile and came out with it. 'Friday the fifth of December – exactly eleven years to the day when I lost Catherine.'

'I'm sorry, Lew,' Madhav said, and looked at the wall clock.

Lewis turned his gaze towards the calendar with its theme of places to go to on Merseyside. 'Strange thing is, this whole month is a carbon copy of that December in 1986. Fifth of December falls on a Friday, just like it did eleven years ago.'

'I think I know what you're driving at, Lew,' Madhav said, and he looked at the coffee table and sighed. 'I think you remembered more of my old theory than you're letting on. Would I be correct in assuming that you're wondering if we could somehow recreate the night Catherine died, we could reverse time to that night?'

Lewis was too choked up to answer, but he nodded twice then poured some more wine. 'Do you think there's any way it can be done?' he asked, with so much repressed pain in his voice.

'Recreating the events can be done; a mock-up of the past can be done – but I think you mean can time-reversal be done. And the answer to that is probably no, it can't be done,' Madhav said, 'but it's getting too late to talk about theoretical physics.'

'Okay,' said Lewis, resignedly, bowing his head.

Madhav felt tremendous sympathy for his friend, and he rose from the armchair and placed a firm reassuring hand on his shoulder. 'Let me have a think about it, okay?'

Well Madhav said goodnight and left, and Lewis hardly slept that night, thinking about the futility of the hare-brained scheme in which he had just involved his good friend. He knew in his heart of hearts that nothing would come of it, but he just had to try something – anything – to see his Catherine again.

At 7pm on the following day, Madhav turned up at the flat, and told his friend that their theoretical experiment was worth a try 'A try, mind you. I can't promise you anything.' Madhav then explained the task at hand. 'I need a lot of information from you. I need to know where everything was in the kitchen – everything single thing – because that's the room we're trying to reverse. I'll have to know everything. What you wore that night, and that includes your aftershave, your thought patterns, and what food was in the cupboards and the fridge, and whether there was washing up to be done in the sink and so on. Okay?'

Lewis thought back to those days of eleven years ago. 'Well, Catherine kept the kitchen bright as a new pin – everything was always spick and span, and there would definitely have been nothing in the sink except a plastic red bowl.'

'Have you still got that bowl?' Madhav asked, in all seriousness.

'It's in the cupboard under the sink,' Lewis recalled with a smile, 'Yes, I still have it. To be honest, nothing's really changed in that kitchen; it's already like a time capsule from the Eighties.

Madhav walked into the kitchen and looked at the fridge magnets. 'Were they there eleven years ago?'

'No, none of them were,' Lewis replied and swiped them from the fridge door. 'This fridge was brand new then, it's never given me any trouble at all after all those years.'

'Was that clock working back then?' Madhav asked, eyeing the ornamental clock built into a giant egg timer on the window ledge.

'Yeah, ' said Lewis, 'that was working okay until a few years ago. I put a new battery in but now it won't work.'

'I'll fix it,' said Madhav confidently. The two men spent well over an hour in that kitchen, going over everything in minute detail. They then went for a meal and Madhav spent most of the time in the restaurant thinking things over. By the Thursday afternoon – the day before 'Reversal Day' as Madhav named it – they had turned the 1997 kitchen back into the kitchen of 1986. Lewis had even painted the kitchen door a magnolia colour and had replaced the handles on the cupboard doors with the same type that had been on them back in 1986, which necessitated a journey to a hardware store. Then Lewis remembered something else from that milestone evening when Catherine had ended her life – and his – the radio in the living room had been playing *Chain Reaction* by Diana Ross. He remembered clearly how the strains of that song had filtered into the kitchen as Catherine lay dying.

'Very good,' said Madhav, jotting down the song title in his notepad.

Then Lewis recalled that there hadn't been blinds in the kitchen that December in 1986; curtains had hung in the window. But what colour were they? Lewis had the heartbreaking task of sifting through folders full of photographs he had taken over the years, and finally found one he had taken of Catherine, showing a huge birthday cake she had baked for her niece. In it she was standing with the cake on a tray, and in the background, Lewis could see that the curtains were plain unpatterned grass-green, and hung from a simple wire. And so, at the eleventh hour, green curtains were bought and strung up on a wire in the kitchen.

Reversal Day arrived – Friday 5 December 1997. Catherine had probably committed suicide between 7pm and 8.30pm that grim evening. Madhav had the tape of Diana Ross set to play in the living room. The lighting in the kitchen and living room was as it was that dreadful day, and the whole reconstruction of the kitchen reopened raw and painful wounds in Lewis's heart. Madhav entered the kitchen with the repaired egg-timer-shaped clock and placed it in the exact position in which it had been all those years ago, on the window ledge. Its ticking was quite noticeable, and heightened the expectations of the two men. They weren't really sure what would happen, but nerves started to get the better of Madhav. At five minutes to six, he left the kitchen with Lewis, and went into the living room. At precisely 7pm, the tape was activated, and *Chain Reaction* played as it had over four thousand days ago in another decade. 'Someone just walked over my grave,' Lewis suddenly whispered.

'How do you mean?' Madhav asked.

'I just had the strangest sensation, like a cold tingling down my spine,' and tears streamed from his eyes. Madhav gripped his arm hard.

Lewis thought: *If Catherine appears, I'll stop her this time, by God I will. I'll save her.*

The longest five minutes either man had ever experienced passed by until sounds of movement were heard in the kitchen. Lewis hurried across the hallway towards the kitchen door and opened it – and there was Catherine, kneeling in front of the gas cooker with her head inside its oven, and she was still moving – still alive.

Even from the living room, Madhav instantly detected the strong smell of gas, and he reflexively put his hand over his mouth and moved towards the kitchen. He saw Lewis on his knees, trying to drag Catherine from the cooker – but his hands went *straight through her* as if she was just some sophisticated hologram. Feeling lightheaded from the gas, Madhav leaned over the sink and threw open the kitchen window, and as he did so, he heard Lewis cry out 'Noooo!'

Catherine had gone, and the gas started to evaporate into nothingness.

The Diana Ross tape in the kitchen was still playing, but outside, two youths parked in a car had the vehicle's radio on at full blast. The sounds of 1997 – *The Drugs Don't Work* by the Verve – filtered into the kitchen through the open window as the last vestiges of 1986 escaped like body heat from a dying person.

A further experiment was planned to recapture the shadows from the past, but Lewis sadly died of a heart attack a month later after sinking into a deep depression. Perhaps the past should sometimes be left well alone.

Our Haunted Skies

I receive a lot of correspondence from people regarding my books and newspaper columns, and in mid-June 2011, I received several emails and letters from readers about a very worrying incident which apparently took place in the skies over Sefton Park on the Sunday evening of 12 June. A Mrs Jenkins was walking her dog along Greenbank Lane at about 8.45pm when she noticed a strange 'cloud' above the trees of Sefton Park. She then realised that the cloud was made up of moving figures in uniform, as well as rolling tanks. She shouted across the road to a Mr Carson, an old neighbour who was returning from his weekly Sunday visit to his sister's, and pointed out the eerie mirage to him. He agreed that the figures and vehicles moving with a gliding motion across the clouds looked like some modern military convoy.

Less than a minute afterwards, the whole ghostly spectacle vanished into the western sky. Two emails were also received from a man named Ernie Shaw, who had been driving down Greenbank Drive near the park with his nephew when the latter pointed out the strange optical illusion over the park. Mr Shaw and his nephew saw only vague humanoid figures, but no tanks, while the author of another email which reached my inbox, a Mrs Stubbs of Mossley Hill, said she and her neighbour had clearly seen the spectral sky-army and 'vehicles' around 9pm that Sunday night. Such mirages may be nothing more than an atmospheric phenomenon that is as poorly understood as the origins of this universe – but in times past, such a sight in the heavens would have been automatically regarded as an omen.

In May 1876, as General George Armstrong Custer and his 600-strong 7th Cavalry Regiment marched off to confront the Sioux Indians, scores of civilians gasped in awe as they saw almost half of the regiment appearing to ride off into the sky. A wise old man informed people this meant that half of that regiment would soon be killed. Little more than a month later, Custer and 264 of his men lost their lives at the Battle of Little Bighorn on 25 June.

Late on the afternoon of Tuesday, 8 January 1901, Frederick Wilde, the landlord of the Prince of Wales pub on Rice Lane, Walton, was drawing the curtains in his parlour when he noticed something quite bizarre in the grey clouds overhead – the eerie image of what looked like a plump old woman in a wedding dress. Wilde drew the attention of six other drinkers to the sinister-looking figure, but only four of them could see it. One of the four said the woman in white was wearing a wedding veil and holding a bunch of flowers. Then the figure slowly faded away. News of the strange vision spread, and a local woman who was to be married in a fortnight's time burst into tears and almost cancelled her wedding, believing that the metaphysical figure foretold her death.

However, a fortnight later, on Tuesday 22 January, at 6.30pm, Queen Victoria passed away at the age of 81. In accordance with the detailed instructions of her will, the monarch was laid out in her coffin in a white wedding dress and veil, with a bouquet in her hand – for that is the way the queen wanted to be dressed when she was reunited with the late Prince Albert, the husband she had mourned for over 30 years. Upon Victoria's death, her son, Edward VII – the Prince of Wales (coincidentally the name of Wilde's pub) became king.

In April 2011 I was inundated with reports of what was described as a glowing blue figure with outstretched arms over Wallasey. Most of the reports claimed the figure appeared on 12 April at around 9.10pm and a majority of the accounts agreed that it was huge, some estimating it to be about 50 feet tall, and hovering a few hundred feet over New Brighton train station. This phenomenon lasted for about a minute, and then the figure vanished. I had quite a few reports from people on the Bootle side of the Mersey who saw the strange apparition over the north-east corner of the Wirral peninsula. Some said it resembled an angel because it looked as if it had wings, but this could have been what other witnesses took to be outstretched arms. There may well be a rational explanation for this apparition – it could have even been ionisation caused by drastic changes in the weather which were occurring at that time, or perhaps some giant metaphysical entity materialised over New Brighton for some obscure reason.

A similar figure with outstretched arms was said to have been hovering over the old Lybro warehouse in Edge Hill in the winter 1972. This figure was seen on a rainy afternoon against grey skies, and unlike the luminous 'Wallasey Angel' this apparition was dark and vaporous, but of similar dimensions (about 40 feet in height). The vision was said by some to resemble a crucified Christ but faded out below the knees. The head and face were barely discernible though.

Several years after this, there was a spate of reports of a giant luminous cross which phased through all the colours of the spectrum as it hovered high above St Mary's Church off Towerlands Street, Edge Hill. These crosses were huge according to the estimates of the many witnesses who saw them (always around midnight) and the average estimate put the length of the crosses at around 300 feet. What their significance was, besides maybe being a symbol of a Christian church, it is difficult to say. Edge Hill is built upon quartz sandstone, and some have opted for the 'earthlights' theory; that seismic disturbances beneath the bedrock of Edge Hill may cause piezoelectric discharges in the atmosphere, creating lightning-like arcs. However, all of the crosses are described as behaving as if they were made of coloured flame, and lasted too long to be a brief electrical discharge.

Another mysterious visitor to the skies of the north-west over the years has been the unmarked black helicopter. In the 1970s there was a plethora of reports concerning these mysterious choppers, and their pilots seemed to pay no regard to aviation laws or to their own personal safety by performing highly risky manoeuvres. Witnesses often saw the helicopters – which were always described as being unusually quiet – flying beneath the high-voltage pylon cables of the National Grid, or swooping beneath bridges such as the Runcorn Bridge. They also made some eerie forays into Liverpool city centre.

In 1972, Michelle, a 21-year-old art student, left her bed to go to the toilet, and happened to glance out the window of her top-floor flat in Gambier Terrace. What she saw sent her running to wake up her flatmates. Hovering in the gaping 'canyon' of the sunken churchyard of St James's Cemetery, which lies adjacent to the

Anglican Cathedral, hovered a black shiny helicopter with dark tinted windows. The machine's rotor blades were a blur and yet the only sound the engine emitted was a low humming noise. The machine hovered stationary about ten feet below the level of the Hope Street pavement over the cemetery below. Three of the students watched the machine for about five minutes, until the helicopter suddenly rose, circled the bell tower of the cathedral, and then headed off towards Wirral.

Just what a high-tech low-noise helicopter would be doing hovering about down in a cemetery at that time in the morning is a great puzzle, unless it was being hunted or perhaps attempting to stay off someone's radar screen by dropping far below the reaches of any radar beams. When Michelle mentioned the strange incident to her art tutor later that day, he warned her to keep quiet about 'such things' and for the next two weeks, the art student and her flatmates were followed by a mysterious dark-blue Bedford van with tinted windows.

Going a little further back in time, to the summer of 1968, a cocky-watchman (whatever happened to them?) was sitting by his brazier one morning at around 3.30am, watching roadworks on the waterfront's Strand Street, when an eerily silent long black helicopter made its way up the Mersey from the mouth of the river in the north, with its undercarriage less than 20 feet from the surface of the waves. The unidentified helicopter swerved silently upwards as it neared the old landing stage, then turned left and flew to a point between the clocktowers of the Liver Building. There the silhouetted chopper hovered for about ten minutes bearing no stroboscopic anti-collision lights or any identifying markings of any kind. The watchman could see that the pilot was obviously up to no good, and when it moved away from the Liver Buildings and hovered towards him, he crouched down in his little canvas shelter. When he looked out about three minutes later, the helicopter had gone.

There were further reports of the clandestine craft days later in West Gorton, in south-east Manchester, where the helicopter hovered close to a block of flats. Several residents turned off their lights and looked out of their windows at the menacing chopper, and some could make out figures at the controls in the cockpit wearing what they described as 'ski suits'. The helicopter then moved to the southeast and was later seen over south Wirral, Chester and North Wales.

In 2009 a mysterious black helicopter was sighted across Merseyside from Birkenhead to Southport. At first, the authorities thought it was probably a military craft from RAF Woodvale, up near Formby, but the type of helicopter described, together with its capabilities, hinted that the chopper was far beyond the usual mundane aircraft associated with that base. This black helicopter was seen to perform right-angle turns over Bootle and fly at what appeared to be supersonic speed across Liverpool Bay. It did not have fins on its tail, and although its body resembled that of a Chinook, it was completely silent. The mysterious craft was seen throughout August 2009, then was seen no more – until December of that year, when it reappeared near the Runcorn Bridge, where it was seen to sweep a blinding beam of light across the Manchester Ship Canal and the West Bank, before taking off at high speed and heading north, where it was lost to sight.

Who or what is behind the black helicopters? Are they merely high-tech surveillance vehicles of the Secret Service, or are they piloted by something with a more sinister agenda?

SEND IN THE CLOWNS

It's strange how the clown, in his painted-on make-up and shiny red tomato-sized nose can be regarded as something very sinister after dark, although I know of many people who just cannot take to clowns, even during the daytime. What is it about the supposedly innocent funmaker that creeps people out so much? Could it be the unnatural white face and heavy eye make-up? Is it this artificiality that can upset some little children when they come into contact with clowns? Some think there is a subtle essence about a figure which, like the sinister grinning-faced joker found in the playing cards, represents a type of humour that goes beyond slapstick hilarity – to the sneering side of comedy. Within all of the books of the Old and New Testament, there is no humour to be found, and many theologians believe there is something about comedy that is linked to the oldest joker of them all – the trickster known as the Devil.

Many years ago in the 1960s, there was a glass case in an amusement arcade at New Brighton where you could insert a penny into a slot, press a button, and watch a life-size mechanical clown in a crimson pointed hat and one-piece red satin costume with polka dots rock backwards and forwards as he pointed at you with his white gloved hand and mocked you with audacious stock insults, before howling with laughter. Young children were terrified of Tickle the Clown, and in 1965 a child in Aigburth died after suffering terrible nightmares about Tickle in the days after a visit to the seaside clockwork comedian.

Seven-year-old Tim told his mother that Tickle was visiting him each night after everyone else had gone to bed. Tim would hear the wardrobe door creak open, and out Tickle would tiptoe, with his finger to his huge red exaggerated lips, warning the boy to remain silent for the coming ordeal – tickling Tim's ribs while the boy lay paralysed on the bed, unable to defend himself. Tickle would sometimes transform himself into a snake, and wrap himself around Tim's neck until he couldn't breathe. Tim was accused of having an overactive imagination as each night he would rush headlong into his parents' room after he had broken free of the clown – but then one night the boy's screams pierced the night and his mother and father rushed into his room to find their lad lying with his head protruding through the rails at the bottom of his bed. The boy's eyes were bulging in terror and he had stopped breathing. His father desperately tried to resuscitate Tim for half an hour, but the boy was dead. An inquest cited natural causes.

Children being frightened to death by bogeymen is nothing new. There is a report in the *Liverpool Mercury* dated 15 November 1887, which describes how seven-year-old Jane Halsall of Churchtown, Southport, was scared to death by a claim that Spring-Heeled Jack was heading for Southport from Liverpool. Jane told her mother about the 'Jumping Ghost', but Mrs Halsall said she had nothing to worry about because Spring-Heeled Jack was dead and buried. The Leaping Terror continued to play on the child's mind though, and she later died from 'congestion of the brain caused by severe fright'.

A month after Tim's death from a night-terror brought on by the real or imagined night-time activities of Tickle the Clown, two children from one of the tough tenements of south Liverpool visited New Brighton, and decided to call in at the amusement arcade where Tickle was on display in his crystal cabinet. One of the boys shoved a penny in the slot and thumped the button, and when they saw the clown rock back and forth, accompanied by his amplified laughter, they didn't even flinch, unlike most of the children who visited the booth. All of a sudden, Tickle seemed to lunge forward and his gloved metallic fist smashed through the glass case, showering the insolent duo with razor-sharp fragments which cut one of the boys on the cheek and mouth. The lads turned and ran out of the arcade in a terrified state as Tickle lolled out of his shattered prison, roaring with laughter.

Strange rumours abounded about Tickle; that he was not a life-size clockwork doll at all, but a demented real-life clown who had murdered someone and was now lying low in the perfect hiding place from the law. Fairground workers swore they had seen Tickle's eyes follow them as they passed his booth when the arcades were closing for the night, and one woman who played the part of a gypsy fortune teller said Tickle had one night waved at her from his glass case as she was going home.

And then, one day in the summer of 1968, Tickle the Clown went missing, and the man who owned the clockwork controversy fell ill and died. When the summer season ended that year and the fairground closed, the locals of New Brighton often reported hearing Tickle's spine-chilling laughter echoing down by the empty arcades, and some even claimed to have spotted the polka-dot clown in his pointed hat, running down towards the pier.

Strangely enough, a clown costume just like Tickle's was allegedly once seen under very mysterious circumstances in Parr,

St Helens. The following account is from an excellent book, published in 1993, titled *Mysteries of the Mersey Valley* by Peter Hough and Jenny Randles – two highly respected researchers and investigators of the paranormal. In their book, the authors mention the 'Clown of Tickle Avenue' and describe a very peculiar incident.

In the 1960s, a ten-year-old girl – named Stephanie by the authors (although this is just a pseudonym to protect her true identity) was playing on Tickle Avenue in Parr, when she and her friend happened to peer through the window of one of the dilapidated houses that were scheduled for demolition on the avenue, when they saw something that mesmerised them: a baggy clown costume of red satin with polka dots with frilly white cuffs, together with a pointed hat, which had a pom-pom sewn into its point, was hanging in an alcove in the house. Only Stephanie and her friend could see it. When the girls called for the rest of their gang to come and have a look at the clown costume, they could not see anything at all, which further deepened the mystery. Stephanie's friend suggested entering the derelict house to take a closer look at the clown's outfit, and so the two girls went into the condemned dwelling, which smelt of damp plaster and mould. In the floor there was a treacherous hole where the floor had given way from the rot. Stephanie reached out across the hole and tried to touch the clown costume, but the out-of-place garment suddenly began to shimmer and promptly dissolved into thousands of ripples. This eerie effect terrified the two girls and they ran screaming out of the house.

Why a clown's outfit should appear in the house in question is unknown, but there is a possibility that Victorian singing clown, Learto, who was a permanent fixture with the local St Helens Grand Circus, managed by Fred Lucas, once lived on the appropriately named Tickle Avenue.

They say that the ghost of that popular clown of the television age, Charlie Cairoli, haunts the Winter Gardens at Blackpool. Cairoli was born in Milan in 1910 but made Blackpool his home until his death in 1980. He once gave a performance in Munich with the Circus Krone, and one of the members of his audience was Adolf Hitler, who later presented Cairoli with a silver watch, but when war was subsequently declared against Germany, Cairoli went to the North End of Blackpool Pier and jettisoned the watch into the sea.

One of the most chilling ghostly clowns I have written about must be Frederick Zozabe, a Czech clown and acrobat who went under the name Zozzaby when he performed in circuses of the Edwardian era. Zozzaby's trademark was his naturally long and pointed nose, which he exaggerated with putty and red paint, and from the 1950s to the present day, the ghost of this clown has been seen in a certain area of Liverpool where Frederick Zozabe committed suicide. He seems to have a penchant for waking children in the dead of night then blocking off their escape route by standing in the bedroom doorway as he roars with laughter and points at his petrified prey. A sweet smell which has been identified as embalming fluid, is always present when Zozzaby puts in an appearance, and sometimes a green aura has been seen around the creepy clown.

In December 2002, two boys – Thomas, aged 13, and his ten-year-old brother, Aaron – were awakened in their bunk beds one morning at 3am, by the sounds of echoing laughter. Thomas looked down from the top bunk and saw a strange partially-transparent man dressed as a clown in a maroon one-piece suit sporting three large buttons. On his head the spectral clown wore a cone-shaped hat, but what stood out most about this apparition was his grotesque and heavily painted face. He had large black gaping holes for eye sockets and his nose was crooked and as red and pointed as a carrot. All around the ghost there was a shimmering curtain of green phosphorescent light. The clown's left white-gloved hand rested on his huge pot belly, whilst the other pointed at the trembling boys and he rocked back and forth, his manic laughter echoing as if he were in a cavern.

The boys were prevented from making an immediate dash from the room because the ghost was blocking their exit. Aaron screamed for his mother but his pleas for help just echoed straight back at him. Thomas slowly climbed down from his bunk and comforted his sobbing young brother, and at this point, the boys could both smell the sickly sweet stifling aroma that seemed to be sucking the oxygen out of the room. Thomas tried yelling for his parents at the top of his voice but for some mysterious reason, his mother and father never heard the cries.

The clown suddenly stopped laughing, which was a relief, but he now wore a horrible grim expression on his paint-plastered face. He pointed to the boys and then curled his index finger in a beckoning gesture, but Thomas and Aaron didn't fancy approaching the clown to see what he wanted. Instead, Thomas grabbed Aaron by the hand, then sprinted from the bed, dragging his hysterical brother with him – and they came within inches of the demonic clown, who roared out an unintelligible word as they brushed past, and tried to grab the boys' collars. Little Aaron felt the large pink furry button of the clown's outfit brush against his face as he lunged past. The children escaped from the bedroom and burst into their parent's room, where Thomas stammered out his account of the scary and outlandish-looking intruder. The parents were worried that a real flesh and blood burglar, possibly even a pervert, was at large in the house, but although they could find no physical evidence of any intruder, they too could not help noticing the sweet sharp smell in the boys' bedroom. This smell had been present when the phantom clown appeared in the same house nearly 50 years before.

On that occasion, two boys, again brothers, awoke in the early hours of the morning to find a man with a skeletal face and long red pointed nose guffawing in the doorway of their bedroom, rocking back and forth and pointing at the brothers just as he did in 2002. On this occasion the two boys made a dash for it and their parents went in search of the clown but came upon nothing in the children's bedroom except a sweet smell that made them feel nauseous. Not long after this incident, the boys' father died, and was laid to rest in an open coffin. The same sweet smell which had hung around the ghostly clown was now evident in the vicinity of the coffin – the smell of embalming fluid. Frederick Zozabe lived at the house which his ghost now haunts, but unlike most ghosts, the clown's supernatural presence is somehow able to get around, for Zozzaby has been seen in the houses of neighbouring streets.

In October 2010, 40-year-old Kelly moved into a terraced house just three doors from the house where Zozzaby lived, and died, in Edwardian times. Kelly had no idea who Zozzaby was, and when she moved into her house she set about decorating the living room first. On the third night at the house, she went to bed earlier than usual, exhausted after scraping the old wallpaper from the high living room walls. Just as she was about to drift off into the realms of sleep, Kelly felt the mattress of her new king-sized bed start to shake. She was puzzled as to what could possibly cause that effect. Then in the semi-darkness she saw that a man was lying next to her on top of the duvet with his head on the pillow. He was facing away from her, towards the bedroom door. As fear gripped her, she noted that the man had on a cone-shaped hat with a rounded tip, and also that he was wearing a ruffled white silk collar and a purplish suit. The man's shoulders were shaking, and Kelly got the strong impression that it was the effect of subdued laughter.

As stealthily as possible, Kelly rolled sideways out of the bed and on to the floor, then quietly got to her feet and ran out of the bedroom and down the stairs, where she turned on the hall light, before taking the bolts off the front door and standing barefoot in her pyjamas on the front step on that chilly October night, staring in horror to the top of the stairs, ready to run at any moment. She thought she saw the shadow of the man who had lain menacingly on her bed, gliding along the landing for a moment.

On the fourth night at the house, Kelly slept with a Bible on her bedside cabinet, but she awoke at around 4am to a sweet overpowering scent that made her feel quite ill, and she had to get up and open the windows to air the room. When Kelly told me about the sweet smell I was immediately reminded of the embalming fluid odour that is often associated with Zozzaby's appearances. To date, Kelly has had no further supernatural experiences at the house, and now has a Bible in every room – just in case.

The land adjacent to the M57 at Gillmoss has been the scene of some very strange goings-on over the years, dating back to the opening of the motorway in 1974. In November 1974, Jeff and Diane Palmer, a couple in their fifties were heading along the M57 (then known by its full title of the Outer Ring Road), bound for their home in Southdene, Kirkby, after a visit to their friend's cottage in Tarbock. It was a calm and unusually temperate November night, with a slight ground mist forming on the fields to the left of the M57 as Jeff Palmer drove his Triumph Stag homeward. The time was around 11.30pm, and Jeff listened to his wife talking about the recent sensational disappearance of Lord Lucan after the murder of Sandra Rivett, his children's nanny, on 8 November. Diane Palmer was speculating about the events that had led up to the murder, when Jeff suddenly interrupted her: 'What's that?' He looked left towards the sprawling misty fields that were sparsely-dotted with lonely-looking trees and the occasional electricity pylon. What seemed to be a pall of faintly blue-green luminous smoke was rolling towards the car from across the fields, displacing the ground mist as it homed in on the Triumph Stag. Within seconds, the strange ball of glowing smoke was on a collision course with the Palmers' car, but at the last minute, instead of crossing the path of the oncoming car, the cloud started to move alongside it, on the passenger side of the vehicle, and Diane Palmer let out a scream, because she could see a huge grinning face in the almond-shaped globular cloud, which was about six feet in diameter with a large crescent mouth on its side, as dark as its eyes. A line ran vertically through each eye, which gave the impression of a clown.

Jeff stepped on the accelerator and was soon doing over 80 miles per hour in order to get away from the gaseous thing. When he looked in his rear view mirror the faintly luminous globe was crossing the central reservation and heading in the direction of a housing estate.

This was undoubtedly an early encounter with the so-called 'Gillmoss Thing' which has since been seen quite a few times on land behind the former bus depot (now owned by Stagecoach).

In July 1982 the same giant glowing face was seen by several motorists driving along the same stretch of the M57. In 1987, the 'Thing' was probably the entity that was encountered by a group of six children who were roaming the fields around Gillmoss during the summer holidays. In broad daylight, the children heard a faint buzzing and crackling sound, and several of them felt their hair stand on end as something brushed past them as they played on the land at the back of Gillmoss Industrial Estate, between the Knowsley Brook and a clump of trees lying adjacent to the M57. Several of the children saw what looked like condensation of some dark vapour in the field after it had passed by, and this was roughly the same size and shape as the globular 'face' that had been seen before in that area. Sensing something dangerous was at large, the children ran off to their homes in Fazakerley and Croxteth.

The true nature of the Gillmoss Thing is open to speculation, although a demonic apparition, not at all that unlike the Gillmoss Thing, was said to have been seen in the vicinity of the Roman Catholic Chapel of St Swithin at Gillmoss when it was being run by Benedictine monks circa 1757. The chapel was, at that time, a converted loft above several cottages, where the Roman Catholic Mass was celebrated regularly. The visiting King of France, and personages such as the Duke de Berri, Commander-in-Chief of the French Army, used to pray at the chapel. Today, we are more prone to search for a rational scientific explanation for the Gillmoss Thing, but in the 1750s, such a phenomenon would have been automatically interpreted as the work of the Devil.